Eamon,

older brother of Jesus

BY

MICHAEL REDMOND

CW00552289

Based on the hit BBC Radio 4 series, this is the first book from Michael Redmond (Father Stone) of Father Ted fame. Michael has been lauded by a number of other well known comedians over the years, in particular Stewart Lee who credits him with the best opening line in stand up comedy...." People often say to me...Hey you, what are you doing in my garden? "

Not many people are aware that Jesus had an older brother named Eamon who was not happy just to stay in the background as the lesser brother of The Messiah. This is his story, taken from the Irish sea scrolls found off the Wexford coast, and of his attempts to emulate the deeds of his younger sibling.

It has also not been documented that the 'Holy' family were originally Irish, both Mary and Joseph having independently emigrated from Ireland to escape the ravages of the mange tout famine which was sweeping across the Country at the time.

They had both joined the Nazareth/Irish Club where they met and fell in love. It is not clear if Mary knew her destiny at the time concerning the Immaculate Conception but there is no doubt that Joseph was unaware that he was later to become the vicarious father of the Son of God.

THE IRISH SEA SCROLLS

Despite much documented evidence, many people are still unaware that the Holy Family was originally from Ireland.

While still in her teens, Mary, the Immaculate Conception, (nee O' Riordan), decided to leave the shores of Ireland to find a better life for herself and managed to find passage on a boat heading east. She arrived in Nazareth about six months later, tired, alone and penniless.

Now, it must be noted that there was only a very small Irish community living in Nazareth at the time but Mary joined the Nazareth/Irish club soon after arriving and it was there that she first met Joseph. Joseph was an immigrant carpenter from Cahirciveen in County Kerry who had emigrated to Nazareth a few months earlier in search of work in the building trade........and the rest, of course, is history.

However, theologians and historians alike, have tended to pay scant attention to the fact that Jesus had an older brother called Eamon....and I have been privileged to recount his story from his Irish Sea Scrolls which I found washed up on a remote beach on the Wexford coast.

THE EARLY DAYS

Eamon was nine years old when his younger brother, Jesus, was born. He had enjoyed a very happy childhood up to then. He had been an only child until the birth of Jesus and although his parents, Mary and Joseph, were by no means wealthy, Eamon was deprived of very little. His father was a talented carpenter and would fashion toys for him from his left over pieces of wood, like little wooden chariots, a spinning top, and wooden soldiers, lots of soldiers. His father had made the full complement of a beleaguered Roman legion who, almost every day, had to face the might of an Army of Catholic, female virgins from Ireland led by the fiercesome Mary, his own mother. The Christ's lived in a modest two up two down house in the heart of Nazareth and Eamon enjoyed the luxury of having his own bedroom until the birth of his younger brother. As soon as Jesus was born, Eamon became acutely aware that the privileged status he had enjoyed in the family up to now was about to change abruptly.

Eamon vividly remembers the day that Jesus was born. He had no idea what a Messiah was or why there was such a hullabaloo surrounding the birth of his brother but it was obvious to him that a Messiah was a very important person who could accord immense and hysterical respect and adoration, even from complete strangers.

He can recall standing in the stable in Bethlehem on that freezing December evening when Jesus was born. He was at a loss to understand why the birth had to take place in a stable instead of the comfort of their own home and quizzed his father about it as they stood around in the stable awaiting the birth.

"That's a good question, son...... "

"So...why? "

"Well, to be honest, I'm a bit confused, myself.....but, apparently, it is so written."

"Written....what do you mean? "

"Well, like, written in the Scriptures."

"What's a Messiah? "

"A Messiah.....he's a sort of a ....a Saviour, I suppose."

"Can I become a Messiah as well? "

"Eh...not at the moment anyway."

"Soon?"

"Not really, no....you can only have one Messiah."

"Oh, why's that?"

"Because.....because he's the son of God."

"You mean, God Almighty?"

"That's right, son, yeah."

"But....if he's God Almighty, surely he can have as many sons as he wants."

"I suppose....em.....he's a very busy man, you see.....he wouldn't really have time to look after more than one child.....and anyway, sure aren't you already my son.....and I wouldn't have it any other way."

"So is God Almighty going to look after Jesus.......is he going to move into the house with us?"

"Not exactly, no....your mother and I will look after him...just like we did you."

Although he had been hailed as the Messiah, it was still a great surprise to all those assembled at the birth that Jesus was able to talk as soon as he was born. It wasn't that he just had the power of speech but he was able to converse in a fluent and intelligent manner. Within minutes of emerging from the womb and as his mother cradled him in her arms, Jesus looked up at her and whispered.....

"Mother."

Mary gaped at her new born baby in disbelief.

"Jesus!......you can talk?"

"Of course I can talk.....I'm the Son of God.....that goat over there..... "

"Yes, Jesus...what about it?"

"It's getting a bit too close for comfort....can somebody ' shoo ' it away?"

"Yes, my child. "

"Are we staying in this stable for much longer?....I

think I may be allergic to hay."

"Not much longer....as soon as the Three Wise Men present you with your gifts, we'll head home straight away."

"Oh yes, the Three Wise Men....my father told me about them.......only two of them are wise, by the way.....the third one is a drunken, half-witted fishmonger from Constantinople who's only there to make up the numbers."

Unfortunately, Jesus's ability to talk at such an early age was a great shock to many people, but none more so than Mrs Kilbride, an elderly widow who lived next door to the Christ's. Mrs Kilbride had been too old to attend the birth in Bethlehem but the following day Mary had left Jesus in his pram in the garden while she attended to some chores inside the house. Spotting the baby in his pram, Mrs Kilbride clambered over the small fence dividing the two gardens and approached the baby Jesus with a preconceived plan to tickle him very gently on the tummy while saying the words.........." Coochi, coochi cooo. ! " As Mrs Kilbride poked her head into the pram to get a close look at the babies' face, Jesus woke from his sleep,
stared at Mrs Kilbride for a few seconds, and said.......

"Who the hell are you?...get your face out of my pram."

Mrs Kilbride unravelled a series of short noises from her throat, indicative of someone who has been badly winded, and then collapsed in a heap on the grass beside the pram. Following Jesus's call for help, Mary found Mrs Kilbride lying on her back on the grass , staring upwards with a look of wide-eyed horror in her eyes. Mrs Kilbride recovered from her ordeal in time but not without developing an unnatural fear of all babies.

As time went on, Eamon became more and more disgruntled with his lot. His schooldays developed into a nightmare. By the time Jesus was only six years old, he was so advanced that he was already in the same class as Eamon even though he was nine years his junior. This was obviously a matter of great personal humiliation for Eamon and he was inevitably on the receiving end of cruel jibes from his class mates.

"Hey, Eamon....is your six year old brother helping you with your homework tonight?"

Both Eamon and Jesus left school at the same time. Eamon was put to work straight away in the carpentry shop but Jesus was allowed the luxury of preparing himself to become a Messiah. He would sit around all day reading the works of great philosophers or hanging out with fishermen. However, Eamon did receive some respite for a year or so when Jesus's teenage years began to kick in. When he was about seventeen or so, Jesus decided it was no longer cool to be a Messiah. He refused to wear his hair long as was expected of a Messiah and began to shun the company of his Apostles. At one point he even went so far as to dress like a member of the Roman Legion as an act of rebellion against his parents, his mother in particular. Things came to a head one day when Peter called to the house one day to discuss his latest parable. When his mother was about to open the door to Peter, Jesus called from his bedroom.

"Tell him to go away."

"What do you mean?....he's one of your trusted Apostles."

"He stinks."

"Jesus, stop that right now."

"He smells of fish...and his hands are all scaly....I'm not coming down,"

Mary had to pretend to Peter that Jesus was

feeling ill and wasn't well enough to compose parables. During Jesus's difficult teenage phase, Eamon was required to stand in as a substitute Messiah for a short while. However, the responsibility didn't weigh very easily on his shoulders. When he was heckled once during a sermon by a Pharisee in the crowd, he waded in and lashed out at the Pharisee, breaking the mans' nose in the process and loosening two of his front teeth. He also attempted without success to alter the tone of some of Jesus's parables. ....the most noteworthy being a ruthless editing of the parable of The Prodigal Son. The Apostles rose up in revolt when he changed the nomenclature of "The Prodigal Son" to " That Jumped-up, Selfish Little Shite. ".

Jesus soon emerged from his teenage phase and began to reclaim the mantle of Messiah. Eamon drifted back in the carpentry shop and whiled his time away fashioning furniture as Jesus's fame began to grow and grow. However, by the time he'd reached his late thirties, Eamon determined that he would begin to make his own mark on life.

Eamons Seafood Shack

Eamon was woken at 7.am by the shrill Irish voice of his mother, Mary, calling him down to breakfast. He lay still for a few moments staring at the ceiling of the small bedroom which he shared with his more illustrious brother, Jesus. He had slept in Jesus's bed that night because Jesus was away on a fishing trip with his friend and apostle, Peter, who helped him compose a parable or two during those often long moments when the fish weren't biting. He had slept in Jesus's bed because it was longer than his bed. Eamon was six feet six inches in height and at full stretch his own bed was not long enough to accommodate the lower six inches of his legs. Eamon was tall and gangly and his legs were totally out of proportion to the rest of his body. In fact, his legs were so long that when he sat down in an armchair, it was necessary for him to part them at the knees if the person sitting opposite him were to see his face. Eamon was thirty-nine years old and deeply resented the fact that he still lived at home with his parents and spent his days toiling away in the family carpentry shop. Other employers were reluctant to take him on because he was Jesus' brother and they didn't want to attract unwelcome attention from the Romans.

However, Eamon had plans of his own and was determined to make his own mark on the world and not remain forever as the lesser-known brother of the Messiah.

"Eamon !..Eamon !.....it's now ten past seven....will you get up out of bed, you dirty big lazy galoot and come down for your breakfast."

The Virgin Mary's voice was so piercing that it could be heard by neighbours' who lived as far as two streets away from the Christ's.

"I'm coming....I'm coming."

"Your bacon will be cold if you don't hurry up."

Eamon arrived downstairs in the small kitchen a few minutes later. His father, Joseph, was already sitting at the breakfast table and was engaged in the delicate operation of piercing the yoke of his fried egg with his fork without allowing the yoke to spill over onto the plate. He liked his yoke to remain inside the little crater which it forms for itself.

"Ah, there you are, son....isn't it a grand day, thank God."

"Is it not raining outside?"

"I suppose it is...but apart from that, it's a grand day."

Mary placed Eamon's breakfast in front of him, comprising of five rashers of bacon, two fried eggs, four sausages, and a mound of black pudding. Eamons' face took on an expression of disgust as he examined the formation of meat on his plate. He delicately pushed the plate away from him.

"I'm..em...not very hungry this morning."

"You're what...not what?....if you think I've slaved over a cooker this morning for you not to be very hungry, you're sadly mistaken...now eat up your breakfast and enough of your nonsense."

"I'll have the black pudding son, if you don't want it....you can never have enough black pudding...very good for the elbows apparently...keeps the bones lubricated, you see."

"Ah,elbows, my granny....now will you both get a move on and finish your breakfasts.......I want the place nice and tidy for when Jesus gets back later."

"I thought he wasn't coming back until tomorrow " said Eamon, as he forced a rectangle of grease-laden bacon into his mouth."

"No, back today, thank God...place is never the same without him."

"And it's never the same whenever Eamon isn't here either." said Joseph, as he delicately placed his hand supportively on Eamons' shoulder.

"But I'm always here."

"That's true, son, I suppose...except wasn't there that time when you were kidnapped by that widow woman, and we were all..... "

"Didn't she kick him out as soon as she realised he wasn't Jesus."

"Thank you, mother...you're always so supportive."

Eamon finished as much of his breakfast as he could manage and reluctantly made his way into the carpentry shop which was adjoined to the back of the house . However, Eamon had his mind on other loftier matters than carpentry on this particular day.

Unknown to his mother and father, Eamon had spent every second of his spare time over the last couple of months working on his plans to set up his own seafood restaurant in Nazareth, and tomorrow was to see the official opening of, "EAMONS' SEAFOOD SHACK.". Eamon felt a surge of pride welling inside him. No longer would people look down on him as Jesus's less glamorous brother, the one who obviously didn't have the wherewithal to become a Messiah, the one who still lived at home with his parents at the age of thirty nine, and who was destined to remain an inconsequential

EAMON, OLDER BROTHER OF JESUS

carpenter for the rest of his life. People would sit up and take notice of him now. Oh yes, he would show the bastards now. He would show them what he was made of. The pioneer who set out on his own and opened the first ever seafood restaurant in Nazareth. People would come from far and wide to eat in his restaurant and would boast about it to their friends later. He would become a national celebrity, noted for the audacity of his exquisite cuisine . Of course, he would not rest on his laurels. He saw how his restaurant empire would expand at breath-taking speed. Soon, he would be opening an, "EAMONS' SEAFOOD SHACK " in Damascus, Abyssinia, and even Rome. Why not, Rome?The Romans would be so taken by his adventurous approach to seafood cuisine that they would forgive him for being the Messiahs' brother and welcome him into their fold. His reverie was interrupted by a knock on the door of the carpentry shop.

"Yes", intoned Eamon impatiently.

The door opened slowly to reveal two teenage girls, about seventeen or so, who entered the shop looking very bashful and apparently trying to stifle their nervous giggling.

"Can I help you?" , asked Eamon, with little in the tone of his voice which would indicate that he might.

"Em....we were wondering if..em...Jesus was in?"

"No, he isn't."

"Are you his brother, Eamon?"

"Yes. "

"My name's Karen, and this is Imelda. We'd love to meet Jesus......we think he's gorgeous."

"What? "

"Lovely eyes, deep and blue as the ocean, his long curly hair, and the way he walks...it's like as if....."

"He isn't here....now piss off.....he's at the doctors having his piles seen to."

"There's no need to be rude, you big long drink of water....no wonder you're not the Messiah..."

When Eamon stood up menacingly with a long saw in his hand, it was more out of deep rooted irritation than any intention to inflict harm on the girls with the instrument, but they fled immediately and Eamon was left alone again in the carpentry shop. Eamon spent the next hour or so half-heartedly shaving pieces of wood in preparation for a contract of five kitchen chairs which the family were providing free to a leper colony. This was an attempt to repair the reputation of Jesus with the large leper population in the Middle East at the time as a result of a botched miracle which Jesus had performed on one of their numbers. A couple of weeks earlier, Jesus had been walking home through the streets of Nazareth following his weekly ' troubleshooting ' meeting with his Apostles. Eamon couldn't stand the word ' troubleshooting ' . He found it pretentious and irksome. However, Jesus liked to use the term at every available opportunity.

"I'm not just a Messiah....I'm also a troubleshooter."

As Jesus was nearing a corner close to their house, he was approached by a woman whose husband was in an advanced state of leprosy. The man had lost one half of his right arm as a result of the disease and his wife pleaded with Jesus to offer her some kind of hope. Jesus was feeling tired and drained after the meeting with his Apostles but took pity on the woman and agreed to accompany her back to her house to see her husband. When they arrived at the house, the man was sleeping in an armchair in the corner of his sitting room. Jesus made to wake the man, but his wife said it was best to leave him be as he found it difficult to sleep during the night. Jesus sat down beside the man and touched him on his diseased arm as he whispered something into his ear. As Jesus got up to leave, he smiled at the woman who at once felt a sense of peace welling inside her. Before Jesus had even reached the door, his wife was astonished to see a healthy new growth forming on her husband's right arm. His arm was definitely growing back again. But the problem was that it didn't stop growing. It kept growing and growing until the mans' arm turned into a huge tentacle which was wandering out of control around the room, knocking ornaments off the shelf and terrifying the family cat who tried to escape by jumping out of a window. The man woke with a start to see his hand drumming on the ceiling of the room in the far corner to where he was sitting . Jesus tried everything in his power but he couldn't will the arm to return to its normal size. When the leper and his wife realised what had happened, they turned on Jesus, screaming insults and obscenities at him and threatening to kill him. Jesus had no choice but to flee for his life.

After an hour or so of wood shaving, Eamons' mind began to drift back to the more pressing matter of the launch of his " SEAFOOD SHACK ". He had devised the menu himself along with his head chef, and he began to recite it to himself, pronouncing each dish with great flourish and pride......."seared scallops in a nest of wild mushrooms"....... "salmon fillets glazed with freshly squeezed limes and lemons (plucked daily from the Garden of Gethsemane) resting in a forest of baby asparagus spears", "mermaids of white, fleshy monkfish (caressed in a sauce of champagne de crème boudoir)" .....succulent sea bass baked in a marinade of virgin seaweed from the Red Sea served with an archipelago of jerusalem artichokes ". As Eamon pronounced the words ' archipelago of jerusalem artichokes ', his father, Joseph entered the carpentry shop.

"Be God, I've never heard of that one before.....an archipelago of artichokes."

"It's just...I was just......"

"An archipelago of artichokes....that's a good one alright......and you could have...you could have a...a peninsula of potatoes."

"Yes, father....I was just day-dreaming."

"Sure there's no harm in that......do you know something.?,.....I could never figure out what the difference is between an archipelago and a peninsula."

"Isn't one where there's a.....no, I've forgotten."

"Sure never mind, life goes on either way. We'll all be sitting down to dinner this evening whether or not we know the difference between an archipelago and a peninsula, and that's what counts."

"True."

"I knew a fella back in Ireland who would spend most of his day, day-dreaming. Imagine that. Seamus Gilfennan was his name...one of the Galway Gilfennans who were very big in the poultry trade at the time. He used to say that it's much better to dream during the day because that way you remember your dreams. I remember meeting him once on the road to Kilternan and he told me that he was stuck inside a giant mango which a few Druids had dropped onto him from the top of a yew tree as he was passing below. I asked him was he day-dreaming?, and he replied that he was. And then he said "Are you interested in joining in the daydream...there's plenty of room for someone else inside the mango ? ". And I probably would have got in with him if I hadn't had a handful of cured bacon in my hand which I was bringing back to my mother for breakfast."

"I see. ......anyway, I'd better be getting...."

"What was it I dropped in to ask you?......ah yes, the chairs for the leper colony. Your mother wants to know how you're getting on with them."

"Tell her they'll be ready on time."

"I'll do that.....see you later for dinner."

"Em....actually, I won't be around for dinner this evening.... a few things to do."

"Oh, you're missing out....steak and kidney pudding this evening...your favourite !...and mine as well, of course. Tell you what, would you mind if I ate your portion since you're not going to be here?"

"No, fire ahead"

"Grand, thanks son."

Eamon had yet to tell his parents about the seafood restaurant. He would have been happy to tell his father, but he knew that his mother would fly into a rage about it and launch a tirade against him for letting the family business down. However, Eamon had already arranged a replacement for himself in the carpentry shop. Dermot, the eldest son of Isaiah the prophet, found that he had no talent for prophesying like his father and had recently completed a night course in carpentry.

Eamon spent that evening putting the final touches together for the grand opening of his, 'SEAFOOD SHACK' the following evening. He arrived home about one o' clock in the morning, tired and exhausted. Jesus was already asleep in his bed, snoring loudly, when Eamon entered their bedroom. He lay on his bed and closed his eyes, expecting a deep sleep to envelop him as soon as his head touched the pillow. However, once again, Jesus's snoring intervened. Eamon tried everything he could to blank out the rasping noise, but it seemed to become more and more persistent. At 4.15 in the morning, still bereft of sleep, Eamons' patience snapped. He jumped out of his bed, fuming and cursing, and took in his hand a jug of cold water which was resting on the dresser. He then positioned himself beside Jesus's bed and held the jug of water a couple of feet over Jesus's face. Eamon tilted the jug slightly to allow the water to decant slowly from it. Jesus woke with a shock as soon as the advance drops of cold water splashed onto his face, but he had not reached a sufficient level of consciousness to understand exactly what was happening to him. He sat up in his bed, shaking his head wildly like a confused dog. He stared at Eamon with a look of initial bemusement which quickly turned to anger.

"What did you do that for?"

"You were snoring again."

"You could have asked me to stop."

"Asked you.!....asked you.!...I asked you about fifteen times, you tedious little Gobdaw."

"Don't call me a Gobdaw...I'm the Messiah."

"Ah Messiah, my Irish Granny."

Eamon chose to break the news about his seafood restaurant to his mother at breakfast the following morning.

"A what?"

"You heard me...a seafood restaurant."

"Over my dead body...what about the carpentry shop..... who's going to run that if you're out gallivanting with your seafood...whatever you called it...answer me that?"

"I've arranged for someone to take over from me."

"Have you now...and who would that be?"

"Dermot...Isaiah's son."

"That lumbering half-wit...how's he supposed to run a carpentry shop when he can't even prophesy to save his own life? ...I can't believe you're doing this to us....after all we've done for you."

Eamon spent the rest of the morning going through the ins and outs of the carpentry shop with Dermot, and left in the early afternoon to preside over the arrangements for the grand opening of the restaurant at 8 o' clock that evening. The restaurant was situated in the unfashionable East End area of Nazareth. Eamon would have preferred his restaurant to be located in the trendy West End quarter but the cost of leasing premises in that area proved to be too expensive. As things stood, he knew he would be put to the pin of his collar to make the monthly repayments on the money he had borrowed from the moneylenders.

As eight o' clock approached, Eamon stood proudly at the door of his seafood shack, dressed immaculately in a brand new purple toga interwoven with gold lace in the shape of a giant salmon, ready to meet and greet his first patrons. However, by 8.30, not even one customer had passed through the doors and Eamon began pacing up and down anxiously. At 8.35, Eamon saw Karen and Imelda, the two teenage girls he had run out of the carpentry shop the day before, approach along the road to the restaurant.

"There you are, Eamon...how's the seafood shack going....any customers?"

"Actually....no."

"Hardly surprising."

"Why...what do you mean?"

"Hasn't Jesus performed another one of his miracles....so masterful."

"Miracle....what miracle?"

"The world and his wife are there."

"Where?"

"Down by the Lake of Galilee......hasn't Jesus given the performance of his lifetime....made thousands upon thousands of fish appear out of nowhere."

"Fillets of cod, salmon steaks and barrel loads of bream to beat the band."

Not even one customer chose to come to Eamons' restaurant that evening. He closed the doors at 10.30 and made his weary way home, disillusioned and totally dejected. As the weeks passed by, only a trickle of customers entered through the doors of " EAMONS' SEAFOOD SHACK ". It became clear that people from the trendy West End quarter of Nazareth were not prepared to enter the East End area where they were likely to be molested and hassled by homeless lepers and gangs of disenchanted youths. Matters came to a head about two months later when a consortium of a chain of Roman seafood restaurants decided to spread their empire into the Middle East and much to Eamons' dismay they chose a prime site in the West End of Nazareth.

Three months later, Eamons was forced to admit defeat and closed his restaurant for the last time. He returned to work in the carpentry shop and was compelled to pay back half his wages each week to the moneylenders.

The Asparagus Famine

Eamon was busying himself by sweeping up loose wood chippings in the carpentry shop when an exotically dressed woman in her mid twenties walked in.

"Hello, are you the proprietor?"

"Well, it's sort of a family business, but I...em."

"Are you, Jesus?"

"No....no, I'm his brother, Eamon. I suppose you're looking for Jesus?"

"No, I don't really follow any religion....I want to place an order for an ornate dining table."

"Oh, I see."

"Did you say your name was, Eamon?"

"Yes, that's right, Eamon"
"Eamon....what a beautiful name."

"Oh...thank you."

"My name is, Azeela."

Azeela had been bought at a market in Abyssinia by a wealthy businessman who took her back to Nazareth as his wife. He was an uncouth, ill-educated man, thirty years her senior, who was given to bouts of drunkenness and oftentimes, violence. Azeela was desperately unhappy with him but she had no means of escape. She knew that if she ran away from him, she would most likely end up on the streets again. Over the following months, Eamon and Azeela began to form a very close relationship. The man who was her husband but whom she referred to as ' my owner ', was away on business at regular intervals and Eamon and Azeela would meet covertly. They became passionate lovers. Sometimes she would stay the night in Eamons' bedroom whenever Jesus was away on tour, other times they would meet on a remote beach by the Red Sea and make love with wild, unfettered abandon. Eamons' heart and soul were surging with freedom and unimaginable joy.

One morning, while Eamon was busying himself in the carpentry shop, his mother burst in through the door wailing on the top of her voice. She took a moment or two to catch her breath before she spoke.

" What is it, mother....what's wrong?"

"Eamon....Eamon!"

"Yes, I'm here....what is it?"

"It's your uncle Frank and auntie Noreen."

"What?......what about them?"

"They were making their way to Nazareth, but they've had all their money stolen in Rome....they're penniless and starving."

Eamons' uncle Frank and auntie Noreen had fled Ireland three months earlier to escape from the asparagus famine which was sweeping through the country at the time. Blanched asparagus spears, gently brushed with extra virgin olive oil, was the staple diet of the Irish at the time and the asparagus blight was causing total havoc. The tragic situation was also being exploited by the Druids who had commandeered any land which was not affected by the blight and were selling asparagus at hugely inflated prices. The Druids were originally a folk band from County Donegal who'd become disillusioned by the music scene in Ireland and had decided to form their own devilish cult which now numbered over two hundred.

Mary placed a bagful of money on the table in front of Eamon.

"What's that?"

"It's a bagful of money...what do you think it is?"

"Well, how?...."

Eamon found himself in a serious dilemma. He had arranged to meet Azeela at their usual spot down by the Red Sea that evening.

"I want you to go to Rome straight away.....I've packed sandwiches and some clean clothes for you. They're in a small town outside Rome called Parithia. They tried to board a small tug leaving Italy for Damascus but the Captain wouldn't let them on unless they paid first."

"How do you know all.....?"

"Because one of the deck hands was an Irish lad from Tipperary and he promised he'd pass the message on to us.....now enough of your questions.....head straight for Damascus and board the first boat to Italy.....there's one due to leave at 2.30 this afternoon."

"But, I can't....I've got a very important appointment tonight."

"An appointment!.......appointment!.....I'll give you an appointment across the back of your ears if you don't get going straight away."

"Why can't Jesus go...why me?"

"Why do you think, you half-brained galloot...because he'd be walking into the hands of the Roman legions, that's why.....anyway, he's working on a very important parable at the moment....he needs some peace and quiet."

"Huh! "

So before heading towards Damascus, Eamon found himself in two minds but decided to make a detour to where she lived. Eamon had never been to the house before but he knew the address. However, fate was against him that day. As he arrived near the house, he spotted Azeela and her husband traveling along the road in his expensive chariot. He made to attract her attention but then thought the better of it. Even if he did manage to get her attention, he could hardly start explaining the situation to her in front of her husband. Eamon left Nazareth with a heavy heart. He knew it would take at least three weeks to travel to Italy and back, and by then surely Azeela would have come to the conclusion that he had deserted her. He tortured himself by imagining her growing sense of hurt and rejection, her pain and anguish, and finally her tearful acceptance that he was gone from her life for good.

Following an arduous boat journey from Damascus, Eamon arrived in the town of Parithia about ten days later. He had never met his uncle Frank or auntie Noreen but his mother had taken the trouble of sewing the name, Eamon, across the front of his toga so that his uncle and aunt would be able to recognise him. Parithia was a very small town and his uncle and aunt, who were sitting in the main square , spotted him immediately as he entered the town. His Auntie Noreen was the first to approach him.

"Eamon....it's me, your Auntie Noreen."

"Oh...hello."

"Look at the size of you....aren't you a great, big strapping lad"

Auntie Noreen grabbed him in a tight embrace and kissed him on the cheek, leaving an unsightly smudge of ruby red lipstick on his face. As she released him from her embrace, Eamon couldn't help but notice that her lipstick had been applied with little expertise and some of it had been transferred onto her two front teeth. His uncle Frank stood behind her, grinning broadly.

"This is your uncle Frank......he's a bit hard of hearing"

"What's that?"

"I say...you're a bit hard of hearing"

"It's OK, I'll have a sandwich later"

"Hello, uncle Frank"

"Call me, Frank"

"Frank..."

"Yes, what is it?"

"Nothing, I was just calling....doesn't matter."

"So how's your brother, Jesus....you must be very proud of him. I could hardly believe it when he was born. Not only did I become an uncle, but an uncle of the Messiah.....I'd be joking to my friends that I have a guaranteed passage into heaven"

"Is that so......"

"Are you a sporting man, Eamon?"

" No, not rea...."

"You have the build of a pole-vaulter....have you done a bit of pole-vaulting ?.....the Irish have always been great pole-vaulters."

"Will you leave the lad alone, Frank, for heavens' sake, can't you see he's tired after his journey......have you got a girlfriend , Eamon?"

"Well, yes....I hope....I mean?"

"Is she an Irish lass "

"No....Abyssinian."

"Oh, the Lord between us and all harm.....Abyssinian... sounds very exotic....did you hear that, Frank.?......Abyssinian."

"Yes, I'm ready when you are....we've a long journey ahead.....your father was a great pole-vaulter."

The boat journey from Italy took nearly three weeks because of rough seas in the Aegean. The boat had to be put to port for over a week on the Greek Island of Corfu until sailing conditions returned to normal and also to enable some repairs to be effected to the hull of the vessel. Unlike many of his contemporaries, Eamon had never holidayed on a Greek Island and would have relished the idea of a week idly spent on Corfu if his anguished thoughts about Azeela were not pervading his mind. He was desperate to return to Nazareth to explain his absence to her and to hold her in his arms once more. To see her eyes smolder as he kissed her fully on the lips and to hear her whisper his name as he caressed the secret contours of her nubile body.

It was late August, and the island of Corfu was still packed with holiday-makers. Corfu was also densely populated by Greek philosophers at the time and sometimes it was difficult to move on the beaches for the amount of tourists sunbathing and Greek philosophers wandering up and down in their togas , stroking their chins and trying to analyse the meaning of life. Sometimes a fight or an argument might break out if an over-exuberant tourist playing beach ball accidentally collided with a Greek philosopher just as he felt he was about to stumble onto some vital universal truth.

It was over four weeks before Eamon trundled back into Nazareth with his uncle and aunt in tow. Mary was at the door of the house to greet them when they arrived. She enveloped her sister in a warm embrace.

"It's great to see you , Noreen.....where's Frank?"

"He's there."

"Where? "

"Frank !....where are....?"

"I'm here."

Frank had somehow positioned himself behind Eamon and his small frame had been totally obscured by Eamons' tall, gangly body. Mary led them into the sitting room.

"Eamon...where's your manners.....I'm sure your auntie Noreens' tongue is hanging out for want of a cup of tea."

"I was saying to Frank earlier....hasn't Eamon got a great look of our uncle Toddy.....image of him....it's the legs, yeah....the long legs."

Without further notice, Noreen lifted the bottom of Eamons' toga to a position above his knees.

"What do you think you're......?"

"Look, what did I tell you, exact same knees....do you see the way they veer a bit to the right..... Uncle Toddy's were the exact same."

Much to Eamons' relief, Noreens' attentions to him were diverted when Joseph walked into the sitting room carrying a large cauliflower in his hand.

"Noreen and....and...and...?"

"It's Frank, you half-eejit."

"Of course, it is.......I've just this minute plucked this cauliflower from the ground to celebrate your arrival."

Eamon slinked out of the room as the conversation began to follow various unlikely themes all connected to the subject of cauliflowers. He was desperate to contact Azeela as soon as was possible. He immediately made his way to her house. He decided that if her husband came to the door, he would present himself as a handyman looking for work .

Eamon waited at the door for five minutes but nobody came to open it. When he entered the carpentry shop the following morning, he saw an envelope on the table with his name written on it. It was a letter from Azeela. Azeela wrote that she could no longer bear living with her uncouth husband and had decided to return to Abyssinia. Eamon was bereft and disconsolate. He once again fell into a deep, undying depression and his behaviour became more and more erratic and unpredictable. One morning, about two months later, Mary entered the carpentry shop to speak to Eamon about some matter.

"Eamon !, Eamon!.....where in the name of God have got to. ?....Eamon !.....Eamon !"

"I'm in here."

"What the....? the Lord save us....what are you doing inside the wardrobe.....have you lost your senses completely this time?"

"I want some peace and quiet."

"Peace and quiet, is it....I'll give you peace and quiet."

Mary began to knock on the door of the wardrobe.

"Go away......I'm feeling depressed."

"I'm not going away till you come out of there."

Disturbed by the noise of Mary knocking on the wardrobe door, Joseph entered the shop.

"Oh sorry, am I interrupting something?"

"Course you're not...your son's feeling a bit depressed so he's locked himself inside the wardrobe."

"Oh, there's nothing worse than a bit of depression. I knew a fella once who used to get so depressed that he'd walk all the way to Constantinople and back until he cheered up...sometimes he'd cheer up when he was only halfway there and he'd find himself in a terrible dilemma...not knowing whether to carry on or come back."

"Ah!...you and your ridiculous stories."

"You see...if he came back and then...."

"Will you shut up for God's sake....Eamon!...come out of that wardrobe now..I need you to finish those wooden oars for Jesus and his fishermen...he has a miracle planned for tomorrow night."

"Well, he'll just have to cancel it."

Eamon didn't emerge from the wardrobe for another two days and Jesus had to improvise with some wooden floor boards in order to perform his miracle.

THE CAULIFLOWER CHILDREN

One day just slipped into another for Eamon as the weeks drifted slowly by. His mind was still on Azeela and nothing else could steal his attention. When he arrived down for breakfast one morning, he noticed his mother gazing furtively through the window towards the house next door. His father, Joseph, was in the garden tending to his vegetable plot.

"No sign of our new next-door neighbours yet."

"How do you know they're arriving today.?"

"Because I make it my business to know, that's why.....hope they keep their garden tidier than the Harrington's...not that that would be hard...useless pair of eejits...weeds everywhere."

"You could have killed them, setting fire to weeds like that."

"And how was I supposed to know they were having sex inside their garden shed.....bedrooms are the place for that....if you like that sort of thing, that is"

Joseph entered the kitchen carrying a very large cauliflower which he'd plucked from his vegetable plot.

"Morning, son....it's good to see you out and about and not inside your wardrobe....are you feeling a bit better?"

"A bit...thanks."

"What do you think of that....isn't she a beauty?"

Joseph proudly held out the cauliflower for Mary and Eamon to admire.

"Yes...very nice, father."

"A beautiful specimen of nature, the cauliflower....mind you, did you know the cauliflower can also be a very dangerous weapon?"

"I didn't.....didn't know that."

"I'll tell you why.....if you were to drop a cauliflower from a height of say.... 85 feet, directly onto a mans' head....he'd get a terrible fright altogether.... because it'd smash on impact, you see, and then he'd look on the ground and think it was his brains scattered all over the place."

"I see."

Eamon busied himself all morning in the carpentry shop, sawing, hammering and polishing his finished articles. He had discovered that work helped to take his mind off Azeela, although there were often moments when her image would suddenly spring into his head as he was fashioning a leg to a new chair and his anguish would be as powerful as ever. Eamon was eating his lunch comprising of crudely made cheese sandwiches and a cup of unpleasantly warm milk when his mother burst into the shop, beside herself with panic.

"Eamon!.....a terrible thing."

"What....what is it....is it, father?"

"What.....what's wrong with your father?"

"Nothing. ....I don't know, you....."

"No, it's not your father.....it's our new next-door neighbours."

"What about them......what's wrong?"

"They're vegetarians, that's what's wrong."

" So?"

"What do you mean...so? ......what do you think?"

"I've no idea."

"Vegetarians as next-door neighbours....what am I going to tell everyone? ......the shame of it.....and I was going to invite them to Christmas dinner next month."

"How do you know they're vegetarians anyway?"

"Haven't they got it emblazoned all over their togas....' NO MEAT HERE '......trouble-makers that's what they are."

When Mary failed to elicit much response from Eamon, she stormed out and left him alone again. Eamon had often flirted with the idea of becoming a vegetarian over the years but because his mother provided meat at every single meal he knew it would be too difficult to put it into practice. Even if Mary was serving afternoon tea and cakes, she would still provide a plate of cocktail sausages to go with it. That evening, Eamon decided to call in on his new next-door neighbours to introduce himself. As a gesture to welcome them into the neighbourhood, Eamon decided to present them with the cauliflower which his father had plucked from the vegetable plot earlier. The door was opened by a guy in his early thirties who seemed lost in thought.

"Hi, I'm Eamon......I live next door."

"Eamon...yeah...cool."

Eamon stood awkwardly in the doorway while his new next door neighbour just stared into the distance. He eventually broke the silence when he couldn't bear it any longer.

"I thought...em..."

"Hey, sorry man...it's just that time of evening...8 o' clock, like to get in touch with whatever energies are in my psychic zone."

"Well...I can always come back another time."

"No...no..come in, man...Sanja."

"Pardon?"

"My name...Sanja."

"Of course...yes...I see."

Sanja led Eamon into the kitchen area. There was a woman, also in her early thirties, sitting at the kitchen table on which a number of small apples, some badly bruised, had been arranged. The woman's arms were outstretched in front of her and her hands were hovering in circular movement a few inches above the gathering of apples, as if bestowing them with some unseen life force. The woman had long, wiry ginger hair from which a plait had been fashioned to run down the left hand side of her body, the head of the plait coming to rest uneasily in a jumble of faded purple, trouser cloth .

"This is my partner, Sunji...Sunji, meet Eamon..our new next door neighbour."

"Eamon!...leader of men."

"No, I'm just a carpenter...my brother, now he's a..."

"Your name...Eamon...it means 'Leader of Men'."

"Oh,really...I didn't know that."

"Didn't your parents tell you?"

"I'm not sure that they knew....I think I was just named after my mother's uncle Eamon who went a bit mad when he was still in his teens and thought he was a horse."

Eamon wasn't aware of it but he was nervously fidgeting with the cauliflower he was holding in his hand.

"What a beautiful cauliflower.. grow it yourself?"

"No, my father grew it....it's a present...for you....I mean, both of you...to welcome you into the neighbourhood."

Sanji and Sunji stared at Eamon for over a minute without saying a word. Eamon began to shift about uneasily from foot to foot, still holding the cauliflower in his hand. Sunji was the first to break the silence.

"We've been waiting for you, Eamon."

"Waiting?"

"Yes ....waiting."

"Oh, em....I could have called in earlier but I...."

"No, what Sunji means is...we've been waiting for you to take us from darkness into light."

"Pardon?"

"Don't you see... ?"

"No, I'm not quite..."

"The cauliflower..... it's not just a vegetable."

"Is it...I mean, isn't it?"

"The cauliflower is life itself....look!...cut through the

outer crust and what do you have?"

"The...em....the inside bit."

"Exactly, Eamon....the inside....a series of paths, canals, if you like....leading to the core, the core of our souls."

The following morning, Eamon entered the kitchen. As usual, Mary was standing by the stove cooking bacon for breakfast. When she turned away from the stove to place some bacon on the table, she suddenly stopped in her tracks. As soon as Mary saw Eamon, she took a deep intake of breath which sounded like she'd just been stabbed by someone in the back. It took her thirty seconds or so before she was able to recover her composure enough to speak.

"Jesus, Me and Joseph!.....Saints of Ireland protect us..... what have you?....Joseph!, come in here immediately."

Mary continued to stare at Eamon, wide-eyed with disbelief. Eamon was dressed in a peach coloured kaftan with the symbol of a cauliflower sewn onto the front. His hair was plaited and he had shaved off both his eyebrows. Joseph entered the kitchen from the garden following Marys' distress call.

"What is it....what's wrong?"

"What do you think? ....your son, look at him."

"By God, son, you're looking very.....dapper...is that the word?...yes, dapper."

"Dapper, my granny….he's only gone and shaved off his eyebrows."

"So, he has…..sure, so what?…I've often wondered what was the point of eyebrows, anyway. If you think about it, they don't really serve any purpose."

"What are you on about?"

"Well, you'd think they might provide a bit of shelter for your eyes from the rain….but not a bit of it…all you need is a slight change of direction in the wind and doesn't the rain blow straight into your eyes….leaving the eyebrowstotally redundant."

"Eyebrows suck the energy from your brain."

"You're probably right there, son…I hadn't thought of that."

"Ah, who ever heard of such nonsense…..I know what's happened!….this has all to do with that pair of looderamawn vegetarians next door, hasn't it?"

"They are not looderamawns, mother, they just happen…."

"I knew it….they've given you some kind of drugs, haven't they?"

"Just because they follow an alternative philosophy in life doesn't mean that they take drugs."

Eamon decided to leave the table before his mother continued to delve further into his new lifestyle. Over the next few weeks, Eamon, Sunji, and Sanji became a regular feature of life on the streets of Nazareth. Each Saturday and Sunday, they could be seen in their peach-coloured kaftans dancing backwards around a giant cauliflower and handing out cauliflower florets to pass-ers-by as an offering of friendship and peace.. They began to attract a large following and within a couple of months, their members numbered over two hundred people, including three Roman soldiers who'd left the Army to join " The Cauliflower Children. ". Sanji decreed that each member should donate their lifesavings to the Sect so that they could buy a large farm together to wor-ship in peace and live in harmony for the rest of their lives. Each member happily agreed to this because they believed that through their continued worship of the sacred cauliflower, they would find ..." THE TRUTH. ".

Eamon could hardly wait for the day when the Sect would buy a farm and all move in together. He con-tinued to be on the receiving end of relentless antagon-ism at home from his mother and he was desperate to escape. Sanji had said he would be welcome to live with them in the meantime except for the fact that "THREE " was uneven and could cause dis-harmony. Mary con-tinued to bristle with rage, not just because of Eamons' lifestyle and appearance, but in particular because a few of Jesus's followers had abandoned Christianity to join the Sect. Christmas was approaching and Mary was planning a big celebration. It was Jesus's thirtieth birthday and Mary had invited a party of over twenty people for Christmas dinner, including The Good Samaritan, and Joshua, the one hundred and three year old, toothless soothsayer. Eamon had always hated Christmas dinner because the conversation inevitably revolved around Jesus and his ' wonderful' achievements. Eamon had played with the idea of spending Christmas day at Sanji and Sunji's but when he called into their house that morning, there was no sign of the couple.He reluctantly returned home to find his mother in a panic as usual about the preparation of the Christmas dinner.

"Now that you're back, you can help with the stuffing for the turkey."

Eamon began to dirty his hands in the kitchen as the invited guests began to arrive at the Christ house. Eamons' uncle Frank and auntie Noreen were the first to arrive followed by the Good Samaritan. Eamon found the company of the Good Samaritan difficult to withstand. His bombastic outpourings about the good deeds he had performed on behalf of others were anathema to Eamon. Mary Magdalene, the woman Jesus had saved from the perils of prostitution, was the next to arrive, closely followed by Joshua, the toothless soothsayer. As they all sat down for their dinner about an hour later, Eamon was appalled to find himself sitting beside the Good Samaritan.

"So, Eamo.....how's the carpentry business these days?".

The Good Samaritans' question irritated Eamon on two counts. Firstly, he hated having his name abbreviated and secondly, he had no interest in the carpentry business.

"Fine, thankyou, Good Samaritan."

"Hey, you don't have to be so formal....call me, Sam."

"Fine, thank you....Sam."

"So, what's all this I hear about cabbages taking over from the Holy Trinity?"

"Cauliflowers."

"Oh....cauliflowers, excuse me."

Eamon felt his blood boil as the Good Samaritan placed a sarcastic emphasis on the words..." excuse me ", and then winked playfully at everyone. Unfortunately for the Good Samaritan, Eamon was holding the jug of hot gravy in his hands at the time and feigning a clumsy transfer of the jug to the Good Samaritan, caused its entire contents to land in his consecrated crotch. The Good Samaritan jumped up from his chair howling in agony and began hopping up and down around the room, backwards and forwards, forwards and backwards, like some demented kangaroo who'd lost its sense of direction. Joseph was the first to intervene.

"Grated lemon on the affected area.....nothing better for a gravy burn....my mother used to swear by it....the whole lemon, by the way, peel, pith and juice...the whole shebang....you'll be as right as rain by tomorrow morning."

While the Good Samaritan retired to the bathroom to apply the contents of the grated lemon to the tenderised skin on his crotch area, the dinner got underway again and the conversation turned to the notable absence of Jesus from the dinner table. Mary wanted to immediately stifle any speculation as to his whereabouts.

"Jesus sends his apologies and blessings to all here but he's decided to go into hiding for the Christmas period. We heard rumours that the Romans had planned to capture him over Christmas....dirty, Pagan hooligans!"

Mary was about to lunge into a diatribe about the Romans but was interrupted by the toothless soothsayer who had entered into a trance-like state and was holding his hands up in the air, an indication that he was 'hearing voices' and was about to make a lofty pronouncement. Unfortunately, the soothsayer was never given any warning of when he would be visited by ' voices ', and it was particularly unfortunate in this case because he had just filled his mouth with a forkful of stuffed turkey and two medium sized brussels sprouts and his lofty words of wisdom were lost in the morass of half-masticated meat and vegetable matter. The soothsayer only regarded his body as a vehicle for ' the voices ' and as soon as he emerged from the trance, he had no recollection of what he'd said. Eamons' uncle Frank came to the rescue.

"I think I know what he said."

"Good man, Frank."

"The only time my father ever spoke was when his mouth was full of food....as soon as he'd swallowed it, you wouldn't get a word out of him........I think this is what the soothsayer said....he said, "For it is written that two false Gods, a man and a woman...they who eat no meat, will enter upon us and promise us salvation from ....I'm not sure of this bit but I think he said....promise us salvation from a root vegetable...but they will be gone as soon as they arrive, leaving many behind with nothing."

"Bullshit!"

"Eamon Christ!.....I don't want to hear that language at Christmas dinner."

The dinner proceeded without any further, notable incidents and as darkness descended on the Christ household, all of the dinner guests with the exception of Mary Magdalene had returned to their homes. Mary and Joseph had gone to bed and Eamon and Mary Magdalene were left alone in the sitting room together. Mary had consumed a vast amount of wine throughout the day and when she tried to unsuccessfully seduce Eamon into having his feet washed, she became angry, confused and deeply offended and began shouting drunkenly on the top of her voice.

"You....you smelly....that's what you are....smelly, middle-aged shyster, you should be bloody flattered that a woman of....of my standing would lower herself by cleaning your stinking feet....you, you...look at you... with yer...yer stupid bloody cauliflowers."

At this point, Mary Magdalene began to make a strange, cackling noise which wavered between laughter and crying.

"You haven't a bloody clue, have you. Your two friends.....what's their names?.......Sanj....Sanj....whatever....I saw them......."

"Saw them?.....saw them where....what are you on about?"

"Saw them stealing off in the middle of the night last night....that's what....with all their belongings.....and some other peoples belongings as well I expect."

Having said this, Mary left the house and could be heard all the way up the street cackling loudly and smashing a wine bottle against a wall. Eamon went to bed and following a very restless sleep, he woke at 8.am, got dressed and went to call on Sanji and Sunji. Once again, there was no response when he knocked on the door. He made his way into the house through a door at the back and found the house completely empty. Not just empty of people but empty of any traces of Sanji and Sunji. They had bolted, along with the savings of Eamon and many other followers. Eamon stood in their kitchen as he felt his heart sink deeper than it ever had before.

It took Eamon three weeks to grow back his eyebrows, but a lot longer to recover from his humiliation.

ARTIFICIAL LIMBS

It was Monday morning and Eamon was feeling particularly low in body and spirit. He'd been on a drinking spree the night before in order to numb the memory of his humiliation at the hands of Sunji and Sanji. He'd drunk at least two litres of wine over the course of the night and had ended up having sex with the widow of a cheese maker who lived on the outskirts of town. He couldn't recall how they found themselves having sex in the large vat she used for churning cheese but he felt guilty about the fact that as soon as she fell asleep, he crawled out of the vat without waking her and made his way home. Eamon was really not in the mood for fashioning pieces of traditional furniture that day.

He looked around at the pieces of timber which lay about the carpentry shop and was suddenly struck by an inspirational idea. It was also an idea which, if it worked, could well upstage some of Jesus's more recent feats. At the end of each working day in the carpentry shop, Eamon often noticed the surplus amounts of wood off cuts which would regularly be thrown away because they either had slight splits in them or were maybe stained by resin and couldn't be used for making furniture. His idea was to use the off-cuts to fashion artificial limbs for the large numbers of the leper community. His heart began to race with excitement as the idea began to gather momentum in his head. He wouldn't have to limit his market to people suffering from leprosy as there were many other people in the community in need of artificial limbs.....maybe as a result of a crash in a chariot race or from falling down a steep ravine while trying to ride their donkey home after a heavy drinking session.

Eamon was disturbed by a knock on the door of the carpentry shop. He opened the door to a man who looked about the same age as himself. It appeared to Eamon that the man must have already been extending his hand in greeting before he opened the door to him, because he immediately felt the crude contours of the mans' opened palm being pressed into his.

"Noel Mahoney."

"Pardon?"

"Noel Mahoney...just moved in next door, myself and the wife....married ten years yesterday...you're not the Jesus fella by any chance, are ye?"

"No, I'm his brother, Eamon...why?"

"Couldn't believe me ears when the wife says to me ...' do you know who are new next door neigbours are?', and I says, ' no, I don't ', and she says, 'none other than the Christs'...'the Christs.?,' says I, 'Yes', she says ....well I could have been knocked down by a....a ...by something very light, anyway....'Are you sure,?' says I, ' Go and see for yourself', says she....and I did and here I am."

"Yes, you are."

"Only arrived from Ireland four days ago and before we know it, we've got the Christs for neighbours....Oh, be God, wait till me brother , Paudie, hears about this... he'll be raging with jealousy, he will...big fan of Jesus, he is...knows every parable off by heart."

"Is that so?"

"How do you manage with the weather here at all?"

"The Weather?"

"Yeah, the heat...does it not kill you?"

Eamon couldn't help noticing that the man was wearing a thick, heavy overcoat.

"Well, it might help if you didn't wear a coat."

"I suppose you're right...it's just that I'd feel a bit strange."

"Strange...why? "

"Well...being outdoors without a coat on....wouldn't feel properly dressed."

"Yes, well anyway, nice to meet you but I'd better be getting on..."

"Don't worry about it, I understand...I'm gone already. I'll pop in again soon, get to know each other even more...sure that's what neighbours are for, isn't it?....there was something else I was going to say to you....what was it I was going to say?"

Noel left a sufficient amount of time to elapse to pressurize Eamon into a response.

"I'm not sure....was it anything to do with poltergeists?"

"Poltergeists?"

"It was a wild guess."

"Oh, I see."

"Do you think it might have started with P...pyjamas... pole-vaulting. ....could they have come into the mix? "

"No, I think you're on the wrong track altogether.....I've got it!....our neighbours back in Ireland...knew them as well as my own mother and father, that's a fact...the Moynihan's...lovely couple...eighteen children....what do you think of that?"

"That's very....em...."

"Right, well, best be off."

Eamon breathed a huge sigh of relief as soon as Noel had left. He nursed a sense of dread that his new neighbour would prove to be very irksome because he was unaware how boring his conversation was and how it could cause other people to experience severe headaches, maybe even leading to a migraine in Eamons' case.

Eamon quickly forgot about Noel as he set about designing his first prototypes for an artificial leg and arm. Fortunately, there were no outstanding orders to be completed in the carpentry shop and Eamon was able to spend almost the entire day playing around with different designs and permutations for his new invention. He was in very high spirits when he closed up the carpentry shop at five o' clock that evening. He couldn't recall ever whistling cheerily to himself after a day's work. In fact, now that he thought of it....he couldn't remember ever whistling ever before in his entire life. He usually found whistling very irritating, but not that evening. He was still whistling as he busied himself in the kitchen at home preparing a pot of tea. His mother entered the kitchen as he was pouring the hot water into the teapot.

"Ah, there you are, mother...good timing...just made a pot of tea."

"What's got into you....never seen you like this before....are you on drugs?"

"No mother....apart from the drugs of my own fertile and ingenious mind."

"Anyway, haven't got time for tea....rushing over to Mrs Isaiah...her husband's just taken a heart attack.....your father's giving me a lift."

"A lift?"

"On his back.....me knee's acting up again."

"I'll make you a replacement."

"Don't try to be smart, Eamon Christ....I'm not in the mood.....now what was it I wanted to say to you?....oh yes....I invited our new next door neighbours over for dinner....give them my apologies for not being here ....I'm sure they'll understand...lovely couple....Noel and Dymphna Mahoney....not like those other two looderamawns we had before them."

"You invited him to dinner?"

"Not just him....his wife as well."

"And....and I'm going to have to sit here on my own with him....with them.....for the whole evening?"

"What are you on about....you're acting like a child...they're hardly going to attack you......Joseph!....Joseph!.....are you ready-....we need to go...straightaway."

Joseph entered the kitchen rubbing his hand on the lower part of his back.

"I'm here...I'm here...don't panic.....I was just rubbing some unguent onto my back."

Joseph bent down on his hunkers while Mary climbed

up on his back.

"It's a good word that, isn't it, Eamon....unguent.....never heard of it before.....saw it written on the tube.....otherwise I would just have called it, ointment."

"It's a great word, father."

Mary began to swing her arm back and forth, her hand striking Joseph on his buttocks each time, in the manner of a jockey whipping his horse into action.

"Will you get a move on...poor Mrs Isaiah is waiting."

"OK, we're off."

Joseph halted for a split second at the door.

"By the way, Eamon...our new next door neighbours are....."

"Yeah...I know."

Eamon dreaded the prospect of spending an entire evening in the company of Noel Mahoney. He had not yet met Mrs Mahoney but he held out little hope for someone who had not only married the insufferable bore in the first place but had steadfastly remained wedded to him for over ten years. A minute or so later, Eamon heard someone knocking urgently on their front door. He opened the door to a woman in her thirties who seemed a bit distraught and whom Eamon noticed had allowed the lipstick on her lips to stray onto her front teeth.

"Sorry to...em....Dymphna Mahoney from next door.....
sorry to disturb you, Jesus, but it's my....."

"I'm not Jesus....I'm Eamon ...his brother."

"Eamon....oh yes, Noel was saying......it's Noel."

"What....what is? "

"He was due back an hour ago and there's still no sign of
him....it's not like him...he's a stickler for time."

"I see....where did he go?"

"Just to the shops ....to buy a bottle of wine."

"OK, don't worry....he's probably just got lost....the
streets of Nazareth can be a bit like a maze if you don't
know them."

"I suppose, yes.....but I'm afraid if I go to look for him, I
might get lost myself."

"Yes, I see what you mean."

"I was wondering if you wouldn't mind....if you could
spare the time, like...do you think you could...?"

Eamon accompanied Dymphna to the nearest wine
shop which was only about three hundred yards away
but in order to reach it, it was necessary to take about
ten different turns. Eamon knew the owner of the wine
shop quite well who greeted him cheerily when they entered the shop.

"Eamon, the man himself....how's it cuttin'?"

"Fine thanks....fine.......em, this is...."

"You've a fair eye for the ladies, Eamon, I'll say that for you."

"This is our new next door nieghbour....Dymphna Mahoney....she's looking for her husband....he went out to buy some wine over an hour ago and still hasn't returned."

"Oh.........what does he look like?"

"A bit like a badger."

The words had shot out of Eamons' mouth before he had a chance to contain them.

"I mean....."

"My husband's about five foot four, stocky, round-shouldered, slightly stooped and has a sort of wispy moustache."

"Sounds familiar.....what was he wearing?"

"A big, thick grey overcoat and...."

"That's the one alright.....he bought a bottle of red.....sweating like a badg....he seemed very hot under that overcoat....it's over a hundred degrees today."

"He doesn't feel dressed without his overcoat."

"By the way, Eamon......is Jesus still operating that water into wine routine?......it's cost me a fortune over the last year or so....can he not do something else instead?....I don't know....maybe....maybe change a digestive biscuit into a piece of prime fillet steak or something?"

"I'll have a word with him, but I can't guarantee any-thing....you know what he's like?"

"Yeah."

It was at least another two hours later when Eamon and Dymphna finally stumbled upon Noel. Eamon spotted him sitting up against a wall in a deserted alleyway off the main thoroughfare. Dymphna ran towards him, her heart in her mouth. His breathing was laboured and he was perspiring profusely.

"Noel....what is it....what happened?....are you alright?"

"I think I fainted......it's the heat...how do they put up with the heat over here?"

"Why didn't you take your big, heavy coat off? ....you must be boiling underneath that."

"I just felt like....it's a shame bringing the coat all the way from Ireland and not making good use of it....it was my fathers', you know."

"I know."

"He'd turn in his grave if he felt it wasn't being made

good use of."

Eamon and Dymphna finally convinced Noel to divest
himself of the coat and Eamon accompanied them back
to their house. Dymphna thought it best if they forgot
about the dinner engagement at the Christs' because
Noel didn't seem fit enough for it, and anyway it was
getting a bit late. Eamon felt sympathy for Noel and his
ongoing plight with his overcoat but he was obviously
secretly pleased that he could now spend the evening on
his own and continue working on the prototypes for his
artificial limbs.

A week later, Eamon met with The Social and Medical
services Dept. of the Nazareth City Council and pre-
sented them with his prototypes for an artificial leg and
arm. The members of the Council were mightily im-
pressed with Eamons' artificial limbs and promised that
they would get back to him very soon. Eamon agreed
to leave the prototype leg and arm with the Council. Eamon was very restless for the next few days. He
found it almost unbearable waiting to find out if the
Council were going to place an order for his prototypes.
There were at least two thousand members of the leper
community in and around Nazareth and most of them
required some form of artificial limb. Four days following his meeting with the Council members, Eamon was
sitting in the carpentry shop enjoying his lunch when
he was interrupted by a knock on the door. Eamon was
convinced that it was Jesus's two groupies again, Karen
and Imelda. They had already disturbed him three

EAMON, OLDER BROTHER OF JESUS

times during the morning because they were planning a " Hairdressing-a-Thon" for charity the following Saturday and were desperately hoping that Jesus would agree to have his hair styled on the day.

"Clear off....I told you already he's not here."

"I'm looking for Mr. Christ....Eamon Christ."

Eamon jumped off his chair and ran to the door to open it. Mr. Bennett, the bald-headed Chairman of the Medical and Social Services stood before him.

"I'm sorry, I thought you were Karen and Imelda."

"Pardon?"

"I mean...bald.....someone else....thought you were someone else...... "

"I see....may I come in?"

"Please do."

When Eamon had seated Mr Bennett, the Civil Servant began his spiel.

"On behalf of, and with regard to, The Nazareth City Council, I, as the representative of the heretofore Body which shall herein be known as The Council, am permitted to formally request that you, Eamon Christ, initially provide forty pairs of artificial limbs, to be used by the Council at their discretion and at a price to be fixed by the two parties involved. "

As soon as Mr. Bennett left the carpentry shop, Eamon punched the air with joy and relief. He had actually received an order for forty artificial limbs. This would only be the tip of the iceberg. Eamon immediately kicked his operation into gear. He would perform his normal duties in the carpentry shop during the day, and in the evening he would set in motion the manufacture of his artificial limbs. He had also enlisted the help of his new next-door neighbour, Noel Mahoney, who had some experience of working in the carpentry trade. By the end of the week, Eamon and Noel had managed to manufacture four artificial arms and two legs between them. Noel had proved himself to be quite a skilled craftsman and was very productive despite the fact that he refused to remove his coat at any point. Otherwise, it is unlikely that Eamon would have been prepared to tolerate his endless and uninspired conversation.

"Isn't it a strange thing, Eamon?"

"What....what's strange?"

"The leper thing."

"Well, what do you mean...it's a disease."

"Oh, I know...I know that, but, I mean, isn't it strange that you don't get any lepers in Ireland."

" I hadn't really given it much thought."

"Figs.!"

"Pardon?"

"Figs....I think it might have something to do with figs."

"I don't quite...."

"People in the Middle East eat a lot of figs.....you'd be hard pressed to find a fig if you were to search the length and breadth of Ireland."

"Figs are fruit...they don't cause disease."

"I'll tell you something...."

Noel paused for dramatic effect before continuing any further. Eamon allowed him twenty seconds or so before impatiently interjecting into his pause.

"What?"

"I'll tell you....I ate a fig a couple of days ago, and do you know what?"

"No, I don't...please tell me."

"I felt very strange altogether.....one of my legs went very wobbly and at dinnertime, I found it very hard to stab my peas with my fork...kept missing the damn things.....what do you think of that?"

"If it's alright with you, I'd rather not give it any further thought."

It had been agreed with the Nazareth City Council that

Eamon was to provide the order of forty artificial limbs in piecemeal, so the following day, Noel and he delivered the four arms and two legs to the Council offices. Eamon was asked if he wouldn't mind waiting for a short while as Mr. Bennett wished to speak to him about some matter. He reluctantly agreed and three minutes or so later, he noticed Mr. Bennett approaching with a small sack in his hand. He seemed somewhat shifty and didn't look Eamon in the eye when they shook hands in the reception area. Mr. Bennett engaged Eamon and Noel in polite small talk as they followed him to his office. When they were seated, Mr. Bennett coughed nervously and didn't look up from his desk as he began to talk.

"Em....I'm afraid we have a bit of a problem....the leg and arm you left with us....the prototypes ...."

"Yes..."

"Well, we...em....fitted the leg to an unfortunate member of the leper community, and....."

"What....and what?"

Mr. Bennett pulled out the prototypes Eamon had given him a few weeks earlier. They were both twisted and mis-shapen.

"Well, it's the heat, you see......the wood started to warp within a couple of days and the unfortunate man lost his footing on some steps and ended up breaking his one good leg.....in the , eh....circumstances, I'm afraid we won't be placing any further orders with you."

Eamon and Noel sat in silence for over a minute as the full gravity of the situation sunk in. Noel was the first to break the silence.

"I can see your point, alright....the heat over here is fiercesome altogether....I was only saying to the wife the other day that...."

"Shut up,. Noel."

EAMONS' ROMAN HOLIDAY

Although many months had since passed, Eamon still found himself pining for Azeela. Sunji and Sanji had managed to distract him for a while as had his business venture making artificial limbs, but as soon as he had time to brood again, thoughts of Azeela began to pre-occupy him. However, at least his financial situation had improved ever since Jesus had wreaked havoc by turning over the money lending House in Nazareth and banishing all its members from town. Eamon was now freed of the crippling debt and repayments he'd incurred as a result of his doomed seafood restaurant. His father, Joseph, took him aside one day in the carpentry shop.

"Listen son...I'd like to hand you a bit of advice....there's only one solution to a broken heart."

Eamon waited over a minute while his father paused for thought.

"A friend of mine back in Ireland....Thomas Casey was his name....no, sorry, I've got it wrong....it was Dermot Neely....Thomas Casey was the one with a broken head....a broken head and a broken heart create two totally different dilemmas altogether. "

"I suppose they do."

"So, anyway, didn't Dermots' wife of fourteen years pack her bags one day and ran off with a pole-vaulter

by the name of Jack Rooney....a terrible Gobshite altogether but you'd be hard pressed to find his match
when it came to pole-vaulting....did I ever tell you I was
a pretty nifty pole-vaulter, myself, in my day?"

"Yes, I think you may have mentioned it once or twice."

"So, after a few months of moping around, Dermot
headed off for a two week holiday in a remote monastery near Killarney and when he came back, wasn't he a
new man.....never spoke another word in his life but he
was as happy as Larry."

Eamon didn't relish the prospect of a few weeks in a
Monastery somewhere but his fathers' words had set
his mind to thinking. A few days later, Eamon hired a
chariot and set off to Rome for two weeks. He found a
pleasant guest house just on the outskirts of Rome and
spent the first couple of days just enjoying the mag-
nificent sites in Rome, sitting idly outside street cafes
sipping coffee and watching the Romans at work and
at play. His spirits were starting to lift and although
Azeela was still not far from his thoughts, he felt his
heart was beginning to heal. On the third day, having spent the morning on a guided tour of the Roman
Senate, Eamon returned to his guesthouse to fetch his
swimming trunks as he'd planned to visit a Roman
Baths in the afternoon. When he entered the foyer of
the guesthouse, he noticed two teenage girls standing
at the reception desk, giggling very raucously to each
other. They had their backs turned to him but just as
he was passing the desk, one of them happened to turn

around. She looked vaguely familiar to Eamon but he was about to carry on upstairs to his bedroom when he heard her calling his name.

"Eamon!"

Eamon didn't know why at the time but he felt an ominous dart striking him in the pit of his stomach. He turned round gingerly.

" It's us.....Karen and Imelda."

Eamon now understood why he'd felt a sense of foreboding.

"We called into your carpentry shop a few months ago."

"Did you?"

"Yeah....we were hoping to meet Jesus...remember? ....think you'd got out of the wrong side of bed that morning."

"And then we met you outside your...em....seafood.... whatever it was called....the time Jesus made all the loaves and fishes appear out of nowhere."

"Oh, yes.....I remember."

"Are you staying here on holidays?"

"Yes, I...."

"Isn't it a small world....we're staying here as well....we're here for two weeks.....we're so excited."

"That's ...em...nice....we'll anyway, nice.... nice to see you again."

"I'm sure we'll bump into each other again....staying in the same guesthouse and all......Jesus isn't with you, I suppose, is he?"

"No, we don't holiday together."

"See ya, Eamon....don't do anything we wouldn't do."

Eamon forced a pained smile as Karen and Imelda giggled their way out of the guesthouse. An hour or so later, Eamon emerged from the sauna room in the Roman Baths and dived straight into the unheated pool running alongside it, revelling in the sudden, tingling surge of cold, clear water washing over him. His enjoyment was disturbed by the sound of playful screaming behind him in the pool.

"Jesus, Mary, and Joseph.......it's freezing, Imelda."

Eamon turned round to see Karen bobbing up and down in the pool, flailing her arms and legs about like some gigantic octopus in distress. He immediately turned his face away and made to slink out of the pool unnoticed by either of the girls. However, Imelda, who was standing at the side of the pool watching the antics of her friend, spotted Eamon as he climbed out.

"Eamon!.....Eamon!...over here."

Eamon granted her a desultory wave of his hand but she

ran towards him.

"It's hilarious....look at Karen.....I told her it was the heated pool."

Karen climbed out of the pool and stood beside them, half-laughing through her chattering teeth.

"You lousy witch....I nearly froze to me death."

Karen then grabbed Imelda by the hand, swinging her around and launching her into the pool.

"Jesus.!....Jesus, help me."

As her exclamations were heard around the pool, Karen playfully pushed Eamon back into the pool and before he had time to compose himself, Imelda had locked her arms around his neck.

"Give me a ' backy ' out of here....I can't bleedin' swim."

Eamon swam the few yards to the edge of the pool and relieved himself of the blancmange of teenage flesh which had suckered itself to his back. As Eamon climbed out of the pool and began to make his way to the changing rooms, he noticed two swarthy looking characters furtively glancing towards him and talking to each other in whispering tones. Eamon dismissed the matter from his mind almost immediately and although he thought he saw the two characters again standing at a distance of fifty yards or so from his guest-house as he made his way out into the balmy, evening air, he certainly didn't let it spoil his enjoyment as he dined in style on a floating restaurant on the Tiber. Eamon went to bed about 11.30 pm that evening and within minutes was lulled to sleep by the expensive full-bodied bottle of Chianti which he had drunk with his gourmet meal. Eamon thought at first that he had been dreaming when a couple of hours later he felt his bed clothes being pulled roughly off his bed and saw two men standing over him. There was a split second moment of terror when the dream turned to reality before one of the men covered his face with a cloth covered in ether. Eamon woke up inside a darkened cell about six hours later. It took a few minutes for his eyes to adjust to the lack of light. He noticed a figure huddled in a corner at the other end of the cell.

"Is it true?.....are you really, Jesus? "

"Jesus?"

"Yes, they say you're, Jesus.....the Messiah.....the Chosen One....the King of the...."

"Alright, alright....I get the message.....no, I'm not, Jesus."

"You're not!.....are you sure?....they said....."

"What do you mean....am I sure?......of course, I'm bloody sure.....if anybody knows who I am, it's likely to be me, isn't it. ....I mean, if I'm not sure who I am....who am I?"

"What's that?....you're going a bit quick for me....I've been in prison a long time.....you're the first person I've spoken to in years."

"I'm not, Jesus......I'm his brother, Eamon.....anyway, who told you I was, Jesus?"

"I heard them saying it when they threw you into the cell.......a couple of Nero's henchmen heard two teenage girls calling you, Jesus, at the Baths."

"Those stupid little bints.! ...... I'm not even like him..... Jesus has a little, chubby face with goofy teeth and a squint in his left eye.....do I look like that?"

"No..."

"I'm six feet four.....Jesus is only four feet ten.....he's a tiny squirt......on sports day at school, he was so small, he used to run under the hurdles."

"I know how you feel....... I have a famous brother as well."

"Really...who?"

"The Emperor, Nero....I'm his older brother, Vinny."

Their conversation was interrupted when the flap on the door opened briefly and their lunches were passed through to the cell. Vinny grabbed his plate eagerly, Eamon less so.

"I can't see it properly in the dark....what do they usually feed you with in here?"

"'Depends what day it is......smells like, 'seafood thermidor' today."

Eamon gingerly placed a forkful of the food into his mouth, and was pleasantly surprised as he moved a morsel of scallop around his mouth, savouring it's soft, velvety texture combined with the richness of the thermidor sauce. He took up his glass and was about to drink from it, but took the precaution of placing it to his nose first.

"Good Lord....is this wine?"

"Yeah, ...probably a Frascati with the fish...although they served us an Orvieto with the mussels last week.....don't favour an Orvieto....bit too dry for me."

"I didn't think prison food would be like this.......is all this because you're Nero's brother?"

"Nah...nothing to do with that.....you're in Rome now....all prison food in Rome is like this."

They both ate their food in silence and when they were finished, sat back and savoured the succulent flavours still circulating in their mouths.

"What do you think they'll do to me?"

"Depends.....if they're convinced that you're Jesus, I'd say you're for the high jump, to be honest with you."

"Well, that's just great....I live in my brothers' shadow all my life, and then die on his behalf."

"At least it's straight to heaven for you."

"Heaven?....you must be joking"

"You what?"

"Don't believe in all that stuff."

"Don,t believe!....but....."

"What if I renounce Catholicism....yes, that would force Jesus's hand...."

"You really don't believe in Heaven and Hell?"

"Course not.....nor in Purgatory or Limbo......I mean, Limbo!....how can anyone really accept that.....tiny babies who die without being baptised are....are banished to this no-man's land somewhere in the galaxy and are never allowed enter the ' Kingdom of Heaven ' because some lunatic hasn't terrorised it by pouring freezing water over its head....there is no life after death, it just doesn't make sense."

"Maybe, you're right."

"So....what will they do with me....throw me to the Lions.? "
"Yeah, probably....that's the usual thing."

"Anybody ever escaped from here....is there any way out?"

"It's easy enough to make your way into the sewers from the prison.....but nobody knows if there's actually a way out from the sewers......it could be a horrible way to die."

"Think I'll take my chances."

Eamon took his chances and escaped into the sewer system the following day. He waded his way through the sewage for a few hours before spotting a manhole just a few feet above him. He managed to clamber up to the manhole which opened with unexpected ease. He was free. It all seemed so easy. In fact, as far as Eamon could remember, it was the only time in his life that an action precipitated by himself had not ended in consummate failure. Eamon arrived back in his parents house a few days later. His mother, Mary, was hosting a coffee morning for the Society of Virgins in her sitting room when Eamon almost fell through the door, weak, hungry and exhausted.

"What the ....Eamon!.....what in the name of God?"

Mary steered Eamon out of the sitting room to avoid any social embarrassment in front of her fellow virgins.

"Look at the state of you....what's that stench.....it's coming from your toga....Saints in Heaven, you're bloody reeking."

Eamon related the story of his imprisonment and his

escape through the sewers of Rome.

"Ah, that explains it."

"Explains what?"

"Didn't Jesus decide to hold a public rally in the square a few days ago....right under the nose of the Romans, and the Roman Centurions didn't even bother him. Peter, the Apostle, heard one of them saying that it couldn't be Jesus because Jesus was in prison in Rome.....isn't it a small world."

"Yeah."

EAMON'S DIARY

It was Sunday morning and Eamon was lying in his bed contemplating his life and his future. He had feigned a stomach upset in order to avoid the ritual of attending Sunday mass with his parents. Eamon found it particularly painful and embarrassing attending Sunday mass with his mother because whenever the priest would enunciate the words...." Jesus. Son of God ", Mary would always shout out in response..." That's my boy. " and then she would place her arm over Eamons' shoulder, turn to the congregation , and say,...."This is my boy as well....a fine carpenter." The bedroom which Eamon shared with Jesus was in some disarray. Jesus had risen at five o' clock that morning because he had to attend a meeting at some secret location outside Nazareth with one of the largest cheese-makers in the Middle East. The cheese-maker was apparently very keen to sponsor some of Jesus's parables. In response to the cheese-maker donating money to Jesus's, 'Poverty Fund', Jesus would agree to an inscription at the top of each parable along the lines...." The Prodigal Son.....a new parable by Jesus....sponsored by ....." CHARLIE THE CHEESE-MAKER....CHEESE TO PLEASE. " The bedroom was in disarray because Jesus and Eamon had engaged each other in a fight during the middle of the night. Eamon often found it impossible to get to sleep because of

Jesus's halo. The luminous, levitating sombrero shone like a beacon in the dark and lit up the entire room and Eamon would often find himself tossing and turning in his bed as sleep eluded him. At times, Eamons' patience would snap and he might end up flinging a pillow at Jesus as he slept peacefully in his bed. If this failed to stir Jesus out of sleep, Eamon would resort to decanting a glass of cold water onto Jesus's face. This would provoke the normally, placid Messiah into a state of blind fury and the resultant fight between the two siblings would leave the bedroom in a state of total dishevelment. However, as Eamon lay in his bed, he was unconcerned about the untidy mess which surrounded him. He was playing with an idea in his mind which he felt might catapult him to fame as a pioneering scribe. Two weeks later, he sat at the small desk in the bedroom he shared with his brother and looked down with great satisfaction at the title he had written for his booklet......."

THE DIARY OF EAMON, OLDER BROTHER OF JESUS

28 A.D MONDAY 14th. DEC.

One of our neighbours, Mr. Gibson, is furious with Jesus at the moment. He was holding a party last night for his wife, Concepta, to celebrate her sixtieth birthday and the entire Irish community in Nazareth were invited to the big shindig. Padraig, the pork butcher, and his wife Bridgeen, who is noted for her unique nose which only sports one large, cavernous nostril, were both there. Padraig is infamous for his unfettered rage and hatred of vegetarians. He is known to place carrots, parsnips, stalks of broccoli etc. on top of a fence in his back garden and throw his butcher's knife at each one in turn until he manages a direct hit. His loud roar of satisfaction can be heard resounding around the neighbourhood whenever he mutilates an innocent vegetable. The " O' BRIEN " clan were also in evidence. Mrs O' Brien had given birth to 19 children over the years but had somehow ended up with twenty children. The story goes that an impoverished single mother, who couldn't afford to clothe or feed her baby, had simply left it beside Mrs O' Brien who was enjoying a picnic along the Lakes of Galilee with her entire family. The woman had then quickly absconded. As soon as the baby started crying, Mrs O'Brien automatically picked him up in her arms to comfort him assuming him to be one of her own. It wasn't until a week later that she noticed there were now twenty children in the house. However, the party was going in full swing when Mr. Gibson noticed that he was running out of wine and because it was already approaching eleven o' clock in the evening it would have been too late to find a wine merchants which was still open. So Mr. Gibson approached Jesus who was on the dance floor throwing himself with gusto into the intricate movements of the latest dance craze.." The Rama Rama Ding Ding ". Jesus is a terrible dancer. Anyway, Mr.

Gibson asked Jesus if he wouldn't mind changing a few bottles of water into a smooth red wine. Jesus immediately agreed but unfortunately something went horribly wrong with the miracle. Jesus did succeed in changing the bottles of water into wine but he also accidentally turned Mrs Gibson, who was standing too close to the bottles of water, into a bottle of Portugese Rose and, try desperately as he did to reverse the process, he couldn't change Mrs Gibson back into herself again. It took ten of us to drag an enraged and heartbroken Mr. Gibson off Jesus as he was about to throttle him. Somehow, Bridgeen, the pork butchers' wife, got caught up in the melee and was screaming on the top of her voice until she managed to remove the handle of a wine cup which had become trapped inside her copious nostril. The bottle of Portugese Rose is being buried four days from now.

28A.D TUESDAY 15TH DEC.

Jesus walked on water today in the small frog pond in our back garden. I have a strong feeling that he's practising for something bigger. He's spending less and less time in the carpentry shop these days and lumbering me with almost all the workload. He ambled into the shop today at around four o'clock in the afternoon complaining that he'd been up all night with Peter, his crude fisherman friend, trying to compose some obscure parable involving a pineapple and a one-legged charioteer from Damascus.

28 A.D WED. 16TH DEC.

A very quiet day today...too hot to do any work. I spent most of the day sitting on my own in the carpentry shop reading the autobiography of Aristotle, the Greek philosopher. I had no idea before reading his autobiography that Aristotle ran a thriving hairdressing salon before throwing it all in for a contemplative life as a philosopher. He was apparently responsible for creating the original " Beehive " hairdo which is so popular with teenage girls in Nazareth at the moment.

28 A.D THURS. 17TH DEC.

I was approached today by a group of disgruntled fishmongers who feel hard done by because none of them were at any time approached by Jesus to be one of his Apostles. The mood among the fish mongering community is that they are more reliable and responsible than fishermen and that they have been openly snubbed by Jesus. They have suggested to me in very strong terms that I should set myself up as an alternative Messiah and appoint fishmongers as my Apostles. I agreed to give the matter some serious thought.

28 A.D FRIDAY 18TH DEC.

Noel, my trusted assistant and neighbour, was rushed to hospital today after collapsing in the street due to the intense heat. It was so grindingly hot that his clothes had become matted to his body and the doctors had to surgically remove his coat with a knife before they could attend to him. I'm not sure how much care they took when they were cutting him free from the coat, but if it is beyond repair I have no doubt that Noel will be disconsolate. I have given up trying to convince him to leave his coat behind in his cloakroom, particularly during the gruelling, hot summer, because I now know that he will never take heed of my advice.

28 A.D SATURDAY 19TH DEC

I'm seeing my new girlfriend, Eileen Maguire, tonight. Eileen is a niece of Isaiah, the Prophet, from the marriage of Isaiah's' sister, Zena, to Martin Maguire, an immigrant Irish plumber. Eileen is a widow woman whose husband died from a severe fever three months ago. My mother deeply disapproves of the relationship. She arrived in the carpentry shop today to ask if I could take a parcel to Jesus this evening. He is hiding out in a remote farmhouse about thirty miles from here as the Romans have issued an edict for his arrest. I told her in no uncertain terms that I had made other arrangements for this evening.

"You're off to meet that harlot again, aren't you?"

"She's not a harlot, mother....she happens to be my girlfriend."

"Girlfriend!....girlfriend , my granny.......her poor husband has hardly settled into his grave yet and there she is....cavorting around with another man...both of you should be ashamed of yourselves...talk of the whole of Nazareth, you are."

"Her husband has been dead for over three months....what do you expect her to do...mourn for the rest of her life?"

" My sister, Concepta, never left her bedroom again after her husband died...fourteen years she stayed inside it until God took her."

"God help me!"

28. A.D SUNDAY 20TH DEC.

Jesus is beginning to attract a huge following to his sermons lately. Ever since he promised the multitudes that whoever shall believe in him will have life everlasting, his popularity has rocketed. I was musing about the idea of eternal life this morning as I fashioned a new dining table for that irritating, smug egotist, The Good Samaritan. I am personally somewhat sceptical about the possibility and nature of an eternal life. Although I haven't had the matter clarified by Jesus as yet, I assume that if a person is living for eternity, therefore that person wouldn't suffer the vagaries of an ageing process. Assuming that to be the case, anyone enjoying the benefits of an eternal life would remain at the same age forever. But that begs the question........." What age are people who live for eternity?". Surely everyone can't be the same age?For example, if everyone is eighteen years old, does that mean you could spend every weekend going out dancing with your Granny? ......or if everyone is fifty five years old, which would signal the end of any kind of skateboarding....except for the odd ,overweight, ungainly eejit trying desperately to regain his youth. The only way eternity makes some kind of sense to me is that you live for eternity at whatever age you die at. This would make eternal life a very enticing prospect for a fit, healthy twenty five year old, but what if you die as a partially sighted eighty nine year old with crippling arthritis and a severe case of irritable bowel syndrome?

28 A.D MONDAY 21ST DEC.

I have an unnatural fear of knitting. If I find myself in the same room as someone who is knitting, particularly if she is one of those women who knit in a relentless, feverish manner, my heart begins to palpitate and if I don't leave the room immediately, I will suffer a panic attack. I can't clearly explain where this fear emanates. I can only assume that being in the presence of someone who is knitting somehow rekindles painful memories of my childhood as I watched with mounting dread while my mother knitted some garment for me which I knew would cause me horrible ridicule as soon as I left the house wearing it. I mention all this because my mother has taken to knitting again and I am forced to retire to my bedroom in the evenings or head out to the local tavern. She is knitting," I LOVE JESUS " socks in various different colours which she hopes to sell in market stalls around the country. The purpose of all this is to raise money in order to buy Jesus a new pair of upmarket sandals. The general view is that Jesus is losing credibility with some of the more upwardly mobile members of his following by wandering around in a pair of old, shabby flip-flops. Needless to remark, nobody even notices that I am forced to walk around in my bare feet most of the time......never mind, flip-flops.

28 A.D TUESDAY. 22ND DEC.

It's almost Christmas and the shopping frenzy is in full swing. It's impossible to turn a street corner without some member of the leper community trying to sell you some cheap Christmas decorations. I noticed in the market stalls today that the latest craze to hit the streets are these solar-powered Jesus dolls who recite the same parable over and over again in an excruciatingly irritating, squeaky voice. Jesus is still paranoid and confused about why his followers have chosen to eat turkey every year to celebrate his birthday. He was quizzing me about it earlier today.

"Why turkey?"

"I don't know.....how should I know? "

"It's not that I ever said that turkey was my favourite dish. "

"It might have something to do with your neck"

"My neck?"

"Yeah."

"Why...what do you mean....what's my neck got to do with it?"

"Well it's...you know....it's quite scrawny, like a turkeys."

"'Scrawny....my neck isn't scrawny."

"It is...it's very scrawny...lots of people mention it."

"Like who?....who mentions it?....I bet none of my

friends ever....."

"Mary Magdalene."

"Mary.!......never! "

"She was here visiting a few nights ago.....kept mentioning your scrawny neck......in an affectionate way though.....she was very drunk.....slurring her words."

"You're just winding me up."

"I'm not....honestly."

"But why turkey?"

"I don't know....there's no point in quizzing me about it."

"God knows what they'll eat to celebrate my death after I die "

"Hmmmm......Eggs, maybe."

"Eggs !....why eggs?"

"Don't know...chocolate eggs...first thing that came into my head."

"Very funny!"

28. A.D WED. 23RD DEC.

Very quiet in the carpentry shop today so I decided to take the morning off and do my Christmas shopping. I thought I was going to have to leave it till Christmas Eve as usual and join the mad throng of last minute shoppers. I really abhor Christmas shopping. People just go insane buying ridiculous things like furry toilet seat covers that mimic the sound of a monkey when someone sits on them and which everyone gives as a present to their uncle Bob who never married and lives alone and therefore always gets silly gifts at Christmas. There must be thousands of uncle Bobs around the world with attics full of furry toilet seat covers, "specialised " scissors for trimming pubic hair (ho! ho ! ho !), aftershave lotions with scents that will drive all women over sixty wild with passion and so on. I suppose the worst thing about Christmas shopping is bumping into people in crowded shopping precincts with whom you are only on nodding terms but who feel obliged to engage you in conversation because it's Christmas. I was cornered by Mrs O'Brien, the laundry lady , as I was trying to exit from a large department store today....

"It won't be long now."

"Pardon?"

"Before the Christmas....won't be long now...only two days away."

"That's true."

"Doesn't seem like Christmas at all, does it?"

"I'm not sure."

"It's all gone far too commercial."

"Has it."

"Oh yes, lost its true meaning.....I don't know why we bother."

"Indeed."

"I mean, it's great for the kids.....they love it....if it wasn't for the kids, I'd be just as happy to sleep through the whole business....and that's the Gods' honest truth."

"I don't doubt the veracity of your statement."

28 A.D THURS. 24TH DEC.

It's Christmas Eve and the carpentry shop is closed for the next three days. Under normal circumstances it would be nice to have the day off but Christmas Eve in the Christ household is one to be avoided at all costs. My mother makes a huge issue of having the house cleaned from top to bottom for " The Christmas ". And because all her time is taken up in the kitchen preparing the food for tomorrow, it's always left to my father and myself to undertake the cleaning chores. In fairness to Jesus, he has always shown a willingness to muck in but my mother refuses to allow him get involved. She is afraid that by kneeling on the cold stone floor to clean it he might damage his knees in some way.

"You can't have a Messiah walking around the place with weak knees. Everytime he stepped on a loose paving stone, it'd be touch and go whether or not he stayed on his feet. Imagine if he was walking on water and his knees went from under him and he ended up skimming around the water on his arse....he'd be the laughing stock of everyone."

It's only 9 o'clock in the evening but I'm off to bed. I've spent most of the day cleaning the house and I'm exhausted. Christmas Day tomorrow and as usual my mother has invited over twenty people for Christmas dinner. Can't wait. !

28. A.D FRIDAY 25TH DEC.

Most people wouldn't bother writing up their diary on Christmas Day . It's 11 o'clock in the evening and I'm sitting at the table in our bedroom listening with growing irritation to the drone and occasional cackle of the dinner guests who still remain downstairs. When I made my excuses and escaped to the bedroom, there were still six or seven guests left. The Good Samaritan was holding court and puffing his chest out with pride as he bored the remaining guests with details of his latest charitable quest. He had cornered me earlier in the day and was attempting to regale me with stories of his crusade in Abyssinia until I accidentally stabbed him in the ear with an opened corkscrew. The relentless tedium of his anecdotes is distasteful enough on its own but this is compounded by the fact that the man suffers from the most objectionable case of halitosis I have ever encountered or ever wish to encounter. Any person who has benefited from his good deeds over the years will have also had to endure the nauseous stench of his breath anytime he came within a few yards of them. I don't know why my mother invites him for Christmas dinner every year because I think even she is growing bored of his tired old stories. Ben Hur, the famous charioteer, was also there. I think my mother invited him for two reasons. Firstly , to impress the rest of the guests that she is on first name terms with him and secondly because she becomes all giggly and flirty whenever there is a charioteer around. Her behaviour became so embarrassing at one point that I felt the need to leave the room. Ben Hur had just finished relating some mildly amusing anecdote which caused the rest of the guests to chuckle politely but my mother threw herself into paroxysms of howling laughter for over two minutes, leaving all the guests to shuffle with rising unease as her cackling seemed to reach levels of hysteria. As I write, things seemed to have quietened downstairs so hopefully they've all gone home. It's all over for another year. Inexplicably, I have a strange but pleasant feeling that I will be somewhere else next Christmas.

For the next couple of months, Eamon wrote up his diary religiously every day. Although he enjoyed writing it, he did not regard it as simply a leisurely pastime. He was determined to have his diary published so that the world would know about Eamon, Jesus's older brother. When the diary was finally completed, Eamon enlisted the help of Noel and between them they managed to write up three hundred copies of the diary within ten days, both of them sometimes working into the early hours of the morning. Within a month, Eamons' diary was in huge demand, however Eamon had seriously incurred the wrath of his mother who hated the fact that snippets of her private life were being exposed to the public and the fact that the diary was distracting the multitudes from the "real" work that Jesus was doing to save their souls from eternal damnation.

"'It's a lot of scurrilous garbage in my opinion......may God the father in heaven forgive you."

"'Well, since he's my step-father, he probably will."

"Don't get smart with me, you cheeky gobhawk....it's far from....from....from....diaries you were reared."

"What?"

"You heard me."

"I did hear you, but I'm still confused.....are some people

reared close to diaries.....of course, I'd forgotten....the diary children....you see them wandering the streets, not a parent in sight, just a diary for company, the lost, empty expression in their eyes, all hope abandoned, as they offer a page of their diary in exchange for a scrap of food."

Mary hated it when Eamon used his intellect to defend himself whenever she launched an attack against him. She turned to Joseph for support.

"Are you going to let him speak to me like that?"

"I had no idea there was such a thing as diary children....by God, you learn something new every day."

"'There isn't...he's making it up."

"Wasn't I stopped in the street the other day and this fella asked me for my autograph...'are you Eamons' father, Joseph?', 'Yes', says I. 'Would you mind signing your name there?' he says.....and he holds a copy of Eamons' diary out to me.....'of course I will', says......"

"Will you shut up and get on with that ironing....if Jesus has to address his followers in a crease-ridden toga, I'll give you an autograph you won't forget."

As months went by, the popularity of Eamons' diary reached unimaginable proportions. Eamon was in a position to employ a full-time manager in the carpentry shop as he concentrated in churning out copies of his diary. Interest in the diary reached Rome and Eamon had to enlist the help of a Roman friend of his to write up four hundred copies of the diary in Roman dialect. Eamon was becoming very wealthy and was in a position to move into an exclusive modern apartment in the fashionable west-end quarter of Nazareth. His lifestyle began to change considerably. He was now a man to be reckoned with, a man who was accorded respect wherever he went. One afternoon in mid-July, almost a full year after a copy of the diary first appeared on the streets of Nazareth, Eamon was happily packing his clothes and other necessities and accessories for his three-week holiday to Egypt when he was disturbed by a loud knocking on the door of his apartment. He opened the door to Vinny, one of his employees who helped distribute and sell copies of his diary. Vinny was almost hysterical

"A pogrom!"

"What....what are you on about?"

"The Romans......"

"What....try to calm down...what about the Romans?"

"They've started a pogrom against anybody found with a copy of your diary."

"What....that....it just doesn't make sense....why would they do that?"

"Don't know....not sure....word on the street is that someones' done a deal with them."

"A deal...what kind of deal?"

"Do you have an uncle Frank?"

"Yeah...he came over a couple of years ago from Ireland....to escape from the asparagus famine......why?"

"The Romans have him in custody....they're going around boasting that they have Jesus's uncle in custody and that Jesus will soon be next."

"But how....how could the Romans have found out that he was in Nazareth....the only people that knew he was Jesus's uncle were me, my father, and my.....my mother....it's all beginning to make sense......she's grassed on my uncle to the Romans in exchange for them suppressing sales of my diary.....un..bloody...believable!"

Soon after, Eamons' fortunes began to plummet. Sales of his diary hit an all-time low, and within a few months, there was no longer any demand for it and it began to pass into history. As winter approached, Eamon realised that he could no longer afford to live in his fashionable apartment and was on the brink of returning to the day to day drudgery in the carpentry shop when he received some exciting news from a recent immigrant from Ireland. Apparently the Pagan community in Ireland, who made up the largest percentage of the population at the time, had received word of the diary and were desperate to read it. Almost immediately, Eamon made up his mind. He had never really been happy in Nazareth. It was time to return home to Ireland.

THE JOURNEY HOME

Eamon woke at 6.am on the morning he was due to leave Nazareth and commence his long journey to the shores of Ireland. Jesus was talking in his sleep as Eamon began to dress himself. Jesus had always been prone to talking in his sleep. Eamon smiled wryly as he listened to his younger brother rambling in his sleep.

"No....I don't....please....no squid......miracle, I know..... loaves and fishes....cod and bream and river trout...no, please...Peter...take the squid away...phobia...no....squid, no squid....squid everywhere, take the squid......!"

Jesus began to scream in his sleep before he woke from his nightmare and sat up in the bed, bleary-eyed.

"What....what happened? "

"It's OK, you were just having a nightmare. ....about squid."

"Oh.....I see."

"Christ!...what's that on the end of your bed.....it's a squid.'

Jesus catapulted out of the bed before he realised that

Eamon was just winding him up.

" Very funny."

Jesus gingerly crawled back into bed and fell asleep again almost immediately. Jesus and Eamon had already said their goodbyes the night before. Eamon finished dressing himself and made his way downstairs to the kitchen. His mother was cooking breakfast for him and his father was quietly drumming out a rhythm on the breakfast table with his two forefingers.

"Morning, son....the big day."

"Morning, father."

"Do you hear that rhythm?"

"Yeah...sort of."

"Irish jig.....if you can dance an Irish jig like your old father used to, you'll have the ladies queuing up for you.....particularly if you can do it wearing your Wellington boots at the same time....don't know what it is but there's something about a man dancing an Irish jig with his Wellingtons on that appeals to all Irish women."

"I see.....I'll remember that."

His mother placed a mound of bacon and sausages on a plate on the table before Eamon.

"You'll need to eat every bit of that....you've a long, long journey ahead of you."

"I'll do my best."

"Are you sure you've packed everything?"

"Yes, mother."

"Toothbrush?"

"Yeah."

"Lots of spare underwear?"

"Hmmmm."

"Your mother's right there, son....don't make the same mistake as me.....when we made the journey from Ireland to Nazareth, didn't I forget to pack some clean underwear....by God, by the time I got to Nazareth, even camels were running away from me....I must have been giving off a terrible stench."

"I've plenty of underwear, don't worry."

"Lubricating oil for the knees....very important."

Eamon listened patiently as his mother and father listed all the various items which they considered necessary for his journey. When he had finished his breakfast, he fixed his knapsack onto the back of the donkey which his parents had bought him for the journey and was ready to leave. He embraced Mary and Joseph warmly, hoisted himself onto the donkey and set off down the street. Noel emerged from his house to wish him a safe journey, still wearing his heavy overcoat in the searing heat. Eamons' route took him round by the Lakes of Galilee. He decided to stop beside the shore of the lake to eat his packed lunch and take a short break. His donkey was supping water from the lake when it was set upon by a man who had apparently been hiding from view behind some large rocks which straddled the lake. The man began to pull the donkey into the lake and was attempting to submerge it in the water when he was disturbed by Eamons' shouting. The man looked up as Eamon ran towards him.

What the hell do you think you're doing?"

"I was just......Eamon...it's Eamon, isn't it?"

As Eamon got close to the man, he recognised him as John the Baptist.

"What are you doing to my donkey?" '

"I was going to baptise it."

"A donkey?"

"Yes, why not?"

"Because..."

"I baptised four ducks this morning....and a stray heron"

"Get away from my donkey, you bloody lunatic"

"Please let me baptise it.....I've baptised all the people in the area who've wanted to be baptised and now there's no one left. If I don't start baptising all the animals, I'll be out of a job."

"Why don't you do something else?"

"Like what?....it's all I'm qualified to do...I don't know anything else.....my mother often told me that I could pour water on peoples' heads even before I could crawl...I'm a natural"

"Is that a dead cow floating in the water?"

"Yes, afraid so....it was an accident...I got distracted by a bald-headed eagle when I was baptising it."

Eamon rescued his donkey from John the Baptist and went on his way. When he looked back, he saw him trying to lure a mountain goat towards the shores of the lake. Eamons' journey was uneventful for the next three days or so. On the fourth night, he set up his tent on a remote foothill of a mountain in Syria. He had just fallen asleep when he was disturbed by a commotion outside the tent. He listened with a sense of rising terror as the front of his tent was ripped open by a large sabre and was confronted by the dishevelled, bearded face of the leader of a gang of feared Nomads known as " The Smellies ". Eamon immediately feared for his life but on this occasion luck favoured him. It transpired that the leader of the Nomads was one, Mick O' Sullivan, a former highwayman from Co. Tipperary who grew up in the same village as Eamons' parents and used to rob local orchards with his father, Joseph, when they were still both kids. Mick O' Sullivan and his band of Nomads offered to escort Eamon through some of the treacherous areas of Syria until he reached the relative safety of the Turkish border.   A few days later, Eamon arrived in the bustling city of Constantinople. In those days, Constantinople was the stronghold of the Welsh before they moved to the west coast of Britain in search of valleys. There wasn't a valley to be found anywhere in Turkey and Eamon could feel the sense of unease among the native Welsh in Constantinople, or little Merthyr Tydfil as it was called in those days. There was nowhere to pitch a tent in Constantinople and Eamon found a small, modest bed and breakfast run by a Welsh woman named Bloddwyn Rees-Jones. Eamon had never seen anyone with such enormous hips in his life. The breadth of her hips were such that she was compelled to turn sideways in order to pass through a doorway.

"'You'll be wanting a room then?"

"'Yes please...just for one night."

"One night, is it?"

"Yes...just one night

"You don't masturbate, do you?"

"No, I'm a Catholic."

"Don't like people masturbating in the rooms, see."

"Yes, I'm...."

"Name?"

"Eamon....Eamon Christ."

"Caught someone masturbating in a room once...threw water all over him....didn't stop him, though...filthy little wanker.....just passing through then, are we?"

"'Yes....I'm on my way to Ireland."

"Ireland, is it? ....you've a long way to go."

"Yes...yes, I know."

"Do you like, pyjamas? "

"Pardon?"

"Pyjamas...do you like pyjamas?"

"Pyjamas....yes, I suppose."

"I love pyjamas, me.....tell you something...if I had my way, I'd wear pyjamas all the time...day and night...plenty of room in pyjamas....you're not restricted, see. .....room nine, second floor."

Eamon had spent a long day on his donkey in order to reach Constantinople before nightfall and was totally exhausted. As soon as his head hit the bed, he was fast asleep. However, his sweet nectar of peaceful slumber was soon to be grotesquely interrupted. It first seemed like a dream, a strange chant inside his head, rising slowly but inevitably to an ear-splitting crescendo. The lounge/bar of the bed and breakfast was situated directly underneath Eamons' bedroom and Bloddwyn and some of her Welsh friends were in full voice blasting out song after song bemoaning the striking lack of valleys anywhere in Turkey.

" Oh, there are no valleys in Turkey

no, no valleys in sight

I like to eat Welsh rarebit

not that fucking...Turkish delight. "

"There are no valleys in Turkey

there's Ankara but no Pontypridd

figs and dates a plenty

but it's valleys, valleys I need.   "

There were about six more verses in the song and every second verse was followed by the same chorus.

"My sex life is all in tatters

not a valley in sight

I need to bare my arse boldly

in a lonely valley at night."

The singing went on and on until the early hours of the morning and when Eamon was woken at eight o'clock by the hustle and bustle outside , he felt like he'd hardly slept at all. Eamon spent little time over breakfast and had already reached the outskirts of Constantinople by nine o' clock. He'd been told of a small port about five miles from Constantinople where he could gain passage on a small cargo ship to Greece. Two days later, Eamon found himself on the Greek island of Crete, lazing on his back on the beach listening to the gentle sighing of the Aegean too-ing and fro-ing on the shore. There were no tourists on the island at the time and the local population consisted mainly of a few ancient Greek philosophers. Philosophising was more or less a 9 to 5 job in those days and the philosophers would spent their day sitting or standing under olive trees, stroking their chins and hoping to come up with some astounding new theory on the meaning of life. Sometimes, they would engage each other in a game of Frisbee-throwing during their lunch break and once invited Eamon to join in on the game. However, Eamon was disappointed when the philosophers decided to call an end to the game after only five minutes or so because they wanted to sit down and ruminate on the true meaning of Frisbee-throwing. Eamon enjoyed his time on the island of Crete but began to get a little bored after a few days and managed to book passage on a ship sailing to the northern coast of Italy. From there he made his way into France which was completely deserted in those days because nobody had taken the trouble yet to learn French. There is no reference in Eamons' notes to indicate how he managed to journey from France to the south east coast of Ireland but he lets us know that he stepped onto the shores of Ireland for the first time on the 21st October.

IRELAND

Eamon arrived in the seaside town of Rosslare around
mid-afternoon. The town was in full swing at the
time because the National vegetable-throwing compe-
tition was just about to begin. Every year around this
time, anybody suspected of being a vegetarian would
be rounded up by the majority, carnivorous population and taken to Rosslare. A three-day Festival would
then ensue during which the vegetarians who had so
far survived the "turnip run", would be tied to trees
in the town and subjected to missiles consisting of a
variety of vegetables being hurled at them. The Festival always opened with the turnip-run. A faction of
specially chosen, sharp shooting meat -eaters would be
positioned on the roofs of all the buildings in the town,
each one equipped with an extra large turnip. The vege-

tarians would then be forced to run through the streets of the town as the missiles of giant turnips hailed down on them. Eamon watched in horror as vegetarian after vegetarian fell to the ground with a nasty, turnip-related injury. This spectacle was his first introduction to Irish culture as it was at the time. Eamon assumed at first that they must be criminals or miscreants of some nature who were being punished for their misdemeanours but he soon learned the truth when he quizzed a large man who was standing beside him watching the spectacle and obviously enjoying it.

"Excuse me?"

"That's a strange accent you have?"

"I'm from Nazareth."

"Nazareth......where in the name of jaysus is that?"

"It's ...in the Middle-East."

"Ah, I see....don't know the Middle East very well....I've always stuck to the south east coast of Ireland meself....are you a pole-vaulter?"

"No....why? '

"If you don't pole-vault, what the hell do you do in the Middle East?"

"I'd need some time to think about that."

"Fair enough."

"Those people....what have they done?"

"Done?.....nothing....they're just vegetarians."

"Is...em...is that a crime here?"

"Course it is....can you name me one vegetarian who's ever made it to the pole-vaulting finals?"

"Probably not...."

"There you are.....I rest my case.....haven't got the strength, you see."

Eamon found the whole spectacle very distasteful and degrading and decided to make his way towards Dublin which was just a medium-sized village at the time of about three hundred people. Eamon mentions in his Irish Sea Scrolls that Dublin was the center of the haute couture industry in those days but supplies us with no evidence to support his claim. It is possible that Eamon was being ironic. However, we do know that Dublin was the centre of the Pagan stronghold and Eamon knew that the Pagan community were the most likely to receive his book warmly. Having travelled through the night on his faithful donkey, Eamon arrived at a small settlement of mud huts near the banks of the river Liffey. There were a few children playing around the settlement, and most of the older children were running about with pole-vaults in their hands and leaping over any available obstacle like a hedge or a woman bent over in the act of washing clothes in a large water barrel. Eamon was tired and hungry and approached one of the women to ask where the nearest bed and breakfast might be.

"Bed and breakfast, you say?"

"Yes....I've been travelling through the night."

"That's a weird accent you have?"

"Yes...I'm from Nazareth....."

"Nazareth!"

"Yes...it's in the Middle E..."

"Oh, you don't have to tell me where it is.....haven't I a cousin over there."

"Oh really?"

"Noel is his name.....heart of gold but the poor lad is a terrible big eejit....wears his fathers' old trench coat all the time no matter what the weather."

"Noel....I know him....he only lived a few doors up from me in Nazareth...used to help me out in our carpentry shop."

"Isn't it a small world? ..... I'm afraid you'll be looking for a long time to find a bed and breakfast around here."

"Well, maybe if you gave me directions it might shorten the search."

"No bed and breakfasts here, I'm afraid......but I'm looking for a lodger at the moment....my last lodger died last week trying to pole-vault across the Liffey.....my name is Mary....Mary the Matchmaker."

Eamon soon settled into life in the mud settlement and even found a job teaching English to the children of Hebrew families who'd come to Dublin from the Middle East to embrace the Pagan lifestyle. Eamon initially found any social interaction very difficult within the mud settlement because it quickly became clear to him that all the women were named Mary and all the men answered to the name of Seamus. There was Mary the Dressmaker ....Midwife Mary.......Man Mary, the transsexual potholer......Mary the Matchmaker...... Maudlin Mary, the Mandolin player......Mad Mary, the Table Support and so on. Eamon was strongly attracted to Maudlin Mary the Mandolin Player. She had long wavy, black hair and mysterious, dark green eyes. Her skin was flawless and her body was shapely, voluptuous and perfectly curved. Were it not for an uncompromising, extrovert wart on the end of her nose, she could have been described as absolutely perfect. It was generally accepted among the community that the mournful, lugubrious airs which Mary played on her mandolin were due mainly to her disaffection with the wart on her nose. Despite the unfortunate wart, Eamon fell deeply in love with Maudlin Mary, the Mandolin Player. Within two months of his arrival at the mud settlement, Eamon and Maudlin Mary had moved into the same mud hut together. When he arrived home from work in the evening, she would be sitting there on a chair in the kitchen, strumming her mandolin and singing in a haunting, plaintive voice.

" The wind whistles above me

under the dark, starry sky

the whispering voice inside me

saying, why, oh why, oh why. "

" I could have been an angel

a flawless Irish rose

why have the Gods left me

with this huge wart on my nose."

As time went on, Eamon settled into a cosy domestic lifestyle with Maudlin Mary. Somehow, his burning desire to achieve notoriety with the publication of his Diary began to slowly dissipate as his past life in Nazareth faded into distant memory. A new life was guiding Eamon from darkness into light and on the 19thOctober, 30. A.D., his life burst into unimaginable joy when Maudlin Mary gave birth to a set of twin boys, Seamus and Seamus.

Printed in Great Britain
by Amazon

85534576R00068